MURDEROUS ROOTS

Dangerous Journeys, vol. 1

VIRGINIA WINTERS

From The River Publishing

Murderous Roots
by
Virginia Winters

Cover art by Karen Phillips, 2017

ISBN: Print: 978-0-9959208-0-4

Sign-up here for my readers' group

❀ Created with Vellum

Chapter One

The phone she held beat an erratic tattoo on her thigh. She steadied it and breathed. Blood thickened where it oozed from the body's nose and out onto the carpet. The pale blue eyes stared into the spreading pool. A long navy skirt covered the body's legs to just above a pair of black flats. Anne knelt, pushing back her own jacket to keep it out of the blood. The hand was cold, and the only pulse she could feel was her own.

The skull was crushed above the right ear. She ran her fingers over the sharp indentation. How she hated trauma. Nausea threatened to overwhelm her, and she sat for a moment, before making the call. The receiver of a telephone dangled from the desk. Best not to touch that, she thought.

Outside, she pushed 911 on her cell.

"Operator, please send the police to the Culver's Mills Public Library. A death."

She went back inside and sat on one of those pale oak chairs that are supplied to libraries. The large clock on the wall ticked on--five minutes, fifteen, twenty. Perhaps she hadn't reached the right operator. Perhaps the police came from Burlington. She put the phone in her purse and leaned back against the wall and breathed and thought about why she came.

Three days before, she slammed the trunk of her new Honda and took a last look round her house. Eloise, her nearest neighbor on the lake and a dear friend, promised to drop in and talk to Albert, her Siamese, as well as to feed him. The young woman who came to take over her practice fitted in with her staff (not an easy task) and was interested in the kind of patients

1

she had. She called this retirement to the world, but she wasn't sure how long she would last without the daily rewards of medical practice.

She was tired. Michael, her husband died two years before. They had no children, and she hoped to carry on in the routine of life would help with her grief. It didn't. Looking after so many children with behavioral and emotional problems took more than she had to give. She realized that she was crawling through her days.

So she was through. Photography, painting, writing, and most recently, genealogy were interests she turned to. Her own doctor encouraged her to take a long leave, try a different lifestyle. She had no money worries. She and her husband both inherited wealth, in her case quite unexpectedly from a heretofore-unknown great aunt. That discovery sparked her interest in genealogy and brought her to sit on this chair, staring at a body. How long had it been? She checked her watch—twenty minutes.

Enough, she thought, as she stood up and walked to the door intending to call again. A police car parked at the curb and a young man ran up the steps of the library, pushed open the main door, and stopped as he reached her at the entrance to the adult section.

"Hello," she said.

"Who are you?"

"Doctor. Anne McPhail."

"Could I see some identification, please?"

Anne handed him her passport and Canadian driver's license.

"What are you doing here?"

"Genealogy research," she said, knowing that he likely didn't understand.

"What?"

"I am looking for my roots, Constable."

"Deputy Graham, ma'am."

"Deputy."

"Could you stay here?"

He walked to the corpse without waiting for an answer.

"Was this exactly as she was? You didn't touch anything?" he asked.

"Nothing."

"I'll have to see your purse and search your car, ma'am."

"That's fine."

He could search her car and her purse all he wanted, she thought, as long as he didn't want to search her. Her dark blue jeans and a casual yellow shirt didn't leave room to conceal any sort of weapon. She hoped he wouldn't insist that she be searched. At least, he wouldn't do that himself.

2

Or so she hoped. The deputy found only the usual assortment her purse contained: car keys, old MasterCard receipts, too many coins, and a lipstick.

More waiting and then came the arrival of several more men, some wearing Sheriff's Office jackets. Crime scene crew, she supposed. A stocky man, dressed in wrinkled khaki pants and a red plaid jacket hurried in. A medical bag proclaimed his profession.

"Hello, Adam. What do you have for me?" the doctor said to one of the men in plain clothes.

Adam moved aside and showed the medical examiner the body on the carpet. The examination was brief but thorough. The real work would be done at the autopsy. The ME turned the head gently to reveal the deep depression in the skull. Odd, Anne thought, no real breaks in the skin. She shuddered again, imagining the blood and macerated brain that must lie below the skin and broken bone.

"What do you think the weapon was, doc?" the detective asked.

"Heavy and smooth, other than that, I'll tell you after the autopsy. Didn't you say a doctor found the body? Where is he?"

"She."

Adam turned towards Anne who stood up and put out a hand to the medical examiner.

"Anne McPhail, Doctor."

"Donald Roase."

He shook her hand.

"Any thoughts?"

"None whatever. I'm a pediatrician. I don't do much trauma, day to day."

The doctor nodded as the stretcher arrived for the body.

"I'll let you know."

The man called Adam spoke to her. "Doctor McPhail, I'm Lieutenant Davidson."

Medium height, tanned, thin, dark eyes, dark hair, straight nose and attractive, but with an edge to it, she thought.

"Hello. Could you tell me, Lieutenant, how much longer you might need me here? I told the deputy what I saw."

As usual, Anne's nervousness made her sound curt and a little abrasive. Knowing her face was flushing a brilliant scarlet didn't help either.

"Could you tell me?"

"Sure."

With a sigh, she went over it again.

"Did you come here by chance?"

"No. I wrote to the librarian here, a woman called Nancy Webb. She told me that her assistant was very good at archival research and would be available today. The lady's name was Jennifer Smith. She is not by any chance—"

"Yes, she is. You've never been here before or written to the deceased?"

"Yes, that's right."

Anne could hear the anxiety in her own voice. He was asking another question.

"How did you find out about the library and Culver's Mills and the records?"

"From the internet. The library is listed as one of the premier sources for early French and aboriginal research in the Northeast. Ms. Webb's name is on the site. My fifth great-grandmother was possibly aboriginal, married to a French-Canadian. My third cousin in Elliott Lake found evidence that he spent time in this area."

She stopped talking as a familiar glazed look came into the policeman's eyes. Not everyone shared her enthusiasm for the minutiae of family relationships.

"Yes, yes," Adam said.

Irritated by his tone, she stood up.

"Lieutenant, I've had it. I'm tired, and I've been sitting on this hard chair for long enough, and I'm leaving."

She had also had it with hard-eyed policemen.

"Where are you going?

"I'm going to Catherine's Bed and Breakfast where a very kind lady is waiting for me. I told her I'd be there before noon. So, if you will excuse me?"

"Dr. McPhail, don't leave town."

Hard to believe but he said it.

"I still have my research to do, Lieutenant."

Deliberately she made it left-tenant and got the look of disbelief that she expected.

The yellow tape, familiar from too many cop shows and too many newscasts, surrounded the building entrance. Her Honda was parked in the library parking lot, across from the fire station. She drove off, aware of the stares of the few onlookers.

A five-minute drive brought her to a grey clapboard house, set back in a flower-filled front yard surrounded by low privet hedges.

A youngish woman, mid-thirties, with tied-back brown hair and intelligent dark eyes answered her knock. Somewhere inside a dog barked an exuberant warning.

"Maggie, be quiet," the lady called back over her shoulder.

"Hello," she said, opening the screened front door, and taking Anne's suitcase.

She took one look at Anne's face and trembling hands and walked her into her large sunny kitchen and prescribed strong tea with sugar.

"I'm Catherine LaPlante," she introduced herself as she put a cup of fragrant hot tea into Anne's shaking hand. "You're Anne McPhail?"

Catherine had the kind of thinness that comes from long hours of hard work, but her smile was sunny and her dark eyes welcoming.

"Yes. Thank you for the tea. I got the shakes on the way over here."

"You're welcome. What on earth happened?"

"I found a body at the library. I'm so cold. Usually, death doesn't affect me this way."

"I am sure the deaths you usually see aren't violent ones."

She poured more tea into Anne's cup.

"Who died?"

"A woman called Jennifer Smith. Someone has murdered her, I think. Did you know her?"

"Oh yes, of course."

Catherine was too shocked to go on.

"I'm so sorry. I shouldn't have been so abrupt in telling you."

"No, what else could you do? You're still shaking," Catherine said, as she got up and put a throw around Anne's shoulders.

"How well did you know her?" Anne asked.

Her gaze moved around the room from the yellow walls and cheerful botanical prints to the dog who watched her intently from her corner under the window.

"Casually, at the library. I haven't had anything to do with Jennifer socially. Do you want to talk about it?"

"Not much. That policeman, Davidson? Is he an intelligent guy? I think he thinks I had something to do with it."

Anne shuddered again.

"Don't worry about his intelligence. He's a bright guy and really fair."

"I hope so."

Anne's voice slurred a little, and her eyelids drooped. Reaction, she supposed.

"Perhaps a nap?"

"Oh, yes."

A nap was what she needed. Odd, how exhausting this all was. The horror of it and her own anxiety, she supposed, as she followed Catherine up the stairs to her room.

~

She woke from her nap with a startled memory of the woman's body lying still on the library floor. Thoughts of leaving immediately filled her mind. Fleeing across the border. She laughed at herself. She came all this way to do some research and if they let her in the library that is exactly what she was going to do.

The scent of fresh coffee dragged her from her lovely room to the kitchen where Catherine was baking.

"Feel better?" she asked. "Would you like some coffee?"

"Oh, yes thanks. Much better, and I would love some coffee. Just milk, please."

She asked Catherine about restaurants in town for lunch and dinner and explained that she hoped she could still do her research.

Catherine directed her to Lil's Diner and suggested that if she liked, she could have dinner with Catherine and her sons.

They agreed on 6:30 p.m. and Anne left for Lil's and the library. The short walk in the sunshine under the bright blue autumn sky lifted her mood until she saw the steps of the library. Nonetheless, this was why she came here, she told herself. Get on with it.

The main section was still taped off, but the stairs to the reference section were open. Her first stop was to speak to the librarian at the reference desk. Both the women behind the long counter seemed to be quite calm, in spite of the terrible event downstairs. Quite odd, she thought. She expected the staff to be too upset to work.

However, one of the ladies directed her back into the stacks to some books on local history. She wanted to learn what had been happening in Culver's Mills at the time her ancestor was supposed to have been living there.

Her own ancestor, the French-Canadian fifth great-grandfather was a voyager, a fur-trader and a soldier. He commanded a fort near the border and acted as a liaison between the French and the Indians. Anne thought he also spent time in Vermont and married there.

She knew that census and church records existed but were scanty for the years she was searching. The librarian had directed her to a tiny old book, the diary of a young French woman who had followed her soldier-husband to the area. She struggled with the archaic French, turning pages slowly, looking for proper names that might be a clue to the people living in Culver's Mills, at that time called Bon Chance.

Many Beauchamp names filled the pages, but in one entry, written in capitals with exclamations was the word scandale. She found the name of a Beauchamp man, Daniel, the word marriage, and what the writer had called a sauvage. The woman must have been baptized because her name was Marie.

However carefully she went over the tightly written pages, she could find no record of LaRonde. She wondered what happened to the Beauchamps. She closed the little volume and handed it back to the librarian.

After her lunch at Lil's, she strolled back to Catherine's. She found her down on her knees in front of a long perennial border.

"Hi, Anne," she said. "I finally had to do something with these. I neglect them, I'm afraid, in favor of the vegetable gardens."

"Oh, let me help," Anne offered and went upstairs to change.

When she came downstairs, she found the policeman waiting for her.

Chapter Two

A dam Davidson watched her leave. She was a tiny woman, blonde with green eyes above a nose that just missed being too large for her square face. Doctor or not, she was the only person seen at the library this morning as far as he knew.

Jennifer Smith had been a fixture in the library since he was a kid. She helped him search through college calendars, teaching programs, and university courses and encouraged him to go to liberal arts at State before Police College. She suggested the night school law courses he still attended.

Why would anyone want to kill her? What did she know? What had she witnessed? Too many questions. Later he would realize he'd missed the important one. What did he know about her?

Like your teacher, your nurse, the doctor, you only saw the tiny professional aspect. Who was she? How did she live? Who did she love, hate? His deputy interrupted his thoughts.

Deputy Graham sat at the computer.

""Lieutenant, look at this. Someone's copied files."

The screen box read download complete.

"What did they copy?"

Computers weren't covered well in Adam's personal database.

"I don't know. We'll get Brad in here. Or maybe Ms. Webb."

"Have you called her?"

"Yeah, she's coming down."

As he spoke an agitated woman burst through the door.

"Adam, what's going on? How did this happen? Who would want to hurt Jennifer?"

Nancy Webb, a tall woman who stood too close, used her height to intimidate. When he didn't move as she loomed closer, she backed away.

"Someone did."

Adam went to high school with Nancy. Didn't like her then, didn't like her now, he thought.

"Is there anything in your files anyone would want to steal?"

"Steal? Our files are book lists, prices, budgets. There is no value in them."

She moved to touch the computer keys but stopped at his warning hand.

"What about personal files?"

She brushed a nervous hand through her cropped, mouse-colored hair.

"I don't keep personal files here, but Jennifer kept her research files for herself and library clients on the network. She worked both here and from home."

"Was a woman called Doctor Anne McPhail a library client?"

"Doctor McPhail. I'd forgotten. She was supposed to meet Jennifer here this morning. She does a lot of her own research, but Jennifer was going to give her access to the archives and help with the local records."

"Where does she come from?" he asked.

"She wrote from Toronto and from a small town somewhere in Ontario. She's retired, I think. Genealogy is one of her hobbies she wrote."

"Did she ask for Jennifer?"

"No, she asked for me. It is my name on the website as the contact person. I suggested the appointment times. Did she find her?"

"Yes, she seemed pretty cool about it."

"She's a doctor. She's hardly going to fall apart, or even let you see her sweat."

Much like you, he thought. What was the relationship between the librarians? Were they friends, enemies, lovers? Too many questions, too little data.

"Did she live alone?"

She stared at the crew removing the section of stained carpet.

"As far as I know."

The stain extended to the floorboards beneath. Nancy turned away with a shudder.

"You didn't know her well?"

"Not in her personal life."

"May I have her personnel file, please?"

"Certainly."

She took him through a door to the left, into her own office, the one with the corner windows, the leather seating area and the flowers on the desk. Mahogany doors concealed the steel filing cabinet that held the employment records. She handed him the one marked Jennifer Smith.

Jennifer worked for the library for thirty years from when she was twenty-three years old. Unmarried. Living at 15 Mill Street in a quiet, not very affluent area of town.

"Do you know who her relatives and friends were?"

She walked to behind her desk and looked out the window at the small crowd gathering on the front lawn of the library.

"She has a sister who lives in Burlington. She sees, saw her at Christmas. I think her name is Darlene, but I don't know her married name. Jennifer didn't like me. We weren't friends."

She turned a suddenly pale face towards him.

"I am going to miss her, though. How can this have happened? What can have been important enough to kill an innocent person like Jennifer?"

She covered her face with her hands, and her shoulders heaved as she lost her self-control.

You're human after all, he thought. A little late.

"We need you to look at the computer and tell us what was copied."

She skirted the patch of carpet-less floor and sat down at the screen.

"This will take a little while if I can do it."

He took another look around the room. A few books, a computer terminal and the card scanner, stood on the high counter of the oak desk. The phone dangled from its cord. Why? Had Jennifer tried to call someone and been struck down as she did? Or had it been knocked off in a struggle? Or used as a defensive weapon?

"Adam," Nancy said, "as close as I can get to it, the download included all fifty-three of Jennifer's clients' files."

"What would have been in them?"

"I suppose personal information, family history and connections, anything she could find about a person's family and its past. Some of these small and others extensive."

"Are they damaged?"

"Oh, yes. An attempt was made to delete them."

"Can you recover them for me?"

He knew he was pushing. He needed a warrant for this sort of material.

"No. I can't give you our clients' personal information just like that."

She had fully recovered her calm.

"I'll see Judge Wilmot."

"You do that, and I'll have your copies ready."

"No, Nancy, our expert will make the copy. In the meantime, give me your keys. we need to secure the building."

She didn't like the idea of handing over her keys, but she did and huffed out the door. He spoke to the deputy leaning against the library desk.

"Dave, you stay here while I see Judge Wilmot. Secure the computer."

"Okay, Lieutenant."

Dave was only too happy to stand, uniformed and important behind the yellow tape.

Adam hurried down the steps of the library, past the little throng of on-lookers and sat in his car to call the judge. This one was going to need a face-to-face explanation. Judge Wilmot held strong opinions about the right to privacy.

The Judge was busy until later in the afternoon, so he drove over to Jennifer's house. The radio broadcasted the news of Jennifer's death. He wondered how long they'd been at it and who called them. There hadn't been any press at the library.

Fifteen Mill St. was a blue clapboard house, set back from the street, no fence, with a flagstone walkway bordered by few early tulips blooming in the beds on either side---early for Vermont in April. He had keys from the drawer in the desk Nancy said was Jennifer's. No purse at the scene.

The door stood open. Backing off, Adam called on his car radio for Pete to join him. Not for him the solo approach. That earned him a bullet in the thigh three years before that took six long months to heal and strengthen. He still felt it in bad .

Pete, Dave Graham's older brother, solid and professional, was Adam's first choice when he needed back-up. When he arrived, they entered the house, service revolvers drawn.

The house was trashed. The search was extensive, destructive, and thorough. No computer downstairs. Why take the computer if you copied the files? Maybe the software was special? Maybe they searched the house before the murder?

"More than one guy did this," Pete said.

"Yeah?"

"Moved refrigerator, freezer, even the stove and washing machine. Those are heavy suckers. Need two guys, or it takes you all day."

"Right. Look for an address book, letters, pictures, anything about family, boyfriends."

"Boyfriends? Miss Smith?"

"Look, Pete."

He found the address book by the phone, and a Christmas card list, birthdays, medical appointments, dental. All paper. She used the computer for everything at work, but all her personal stuff lay here in plain sight, not in a computer file, and all intact. He found a Darlene Utronski with a Burlington phone number.

Most of the other addresses were local people in the service industries or professions. She had been involved in volunteer organizations: the hospital, the high school, and he remembered the local little theatre.

Her furniture and her clothes were all small-town professional, no dramatic flair, nothing out of the ordinary. The top of an old upright piano held family pictures---one of her sister he supposed, with her husband and three kid and another a wedding picture, the bride and groom in old-fashioned clothes, her parents' wedding, likely.

Cables snaked from a power bar to a desk in the second bedroom. No computer and no file cabinet here. She probably kept all her work on the computer, he thought.

The crackle of Pete's shoulder radio interrupted the search. He was needed out on the main highway for a four-car collision. This search could be continued later. For now, Adam was going to call on Anne McPhail.

Chapter Three

Catherine's Bed and Breakfast, est.1983 asserted the little folk-art sign in front of the rambling clapboard house. Catherine, a Canadian who came to Vermont to marry Greg LaPlante. Greg liked fast cars and Canadian Rye as well as he liked Canadian women, a combination that killed him in the second year of their marriage, leaving her with twin boys, no money, an old house, and a lot of energy. Bed and breakfast fed, housed and clothed them ever since. The boys were sixteen now, and luckily like their mother, not their fiery dad, except for red hair, freckles and a love for football.

And football it was on the front lawn as Adam pulled up.

"Hey, Lieutenant Davidson."

"Hey, guys. How's it going?"

He passed them with a casual wave and walked up the steps of the white-painted porch. Their mother met him at the door.

"Hello, Adam. This is so awful."

She smiled at him but with worry on her thin features. She still bore the flat a's of Canada in her voice.

"Do you want Dr. McPhail?" she asked as she held open the screen door.

"Yes, I do."

She called to Anne as she showed Adam to the small front sitting room.

"Lieutenant Davidson is here, Anne."

"Thank you."

She walked into the room and sat down in a green wingback chair across from Adam.

"When did you arrive in Culver's Mills, Dr. McPhail?"

"About 9:30am. I had a coffee at Tim Horton's off the highway because I was too early for my appointment. Then I drove into town. The counter girl told me how to find the library."

She tried not to twist her fingers into knots, a habit when she was nervous.

"What time did you cross the border?"

"At 8:00am. I crossed at Thousand Islands and drove through New York. They scanned my passport, of course, so the time should show if that is important."

She knew it was important. How could she dig herself out of this unless this policeman realized the woman was many hours dead by the time she crossed the border? Surely the Medical Examiner was as competent as he had looked at the library.

He watched her face. Was she what she seemed, a pleasant, intelligent middle-aged professional, in this mess by accident?

"Has the medical examiner determined the time of death?" she asked, anxiety putting a little edge on her tone.

"Not yet. Do you have an opinion?"

"I'm a pediatrician. Death is not something we have a lot of experience with, not violent death at any rate. But I did notice her blood was clotted, and her hand was cold and stiff when I tried for a pulse. Hours dead, I thought at the time. Why would she have been in the library so early - unless she hadn't left the night before?"

In spite of herself, Anne was interested in the crime as a mystery. Too much Agatha Christie and Rex Stout.

"That's a good thought, doctor. What can you tell me about genealogy programs?"

She looked at him in surprise.

"Only the one I use. It's called Reunion. I use it to record information as I find it."

"Does everyone who—what?—studies genealogy use a computer?"

"Most people do now. There is so much information online that not using one would really hamper you."

"And would someone like Jennifer Smith use the same program

"Possibly. She was a professional. It would depend on how many clients she had, and how much she needed to store and cross-reference. She would use other programs also, for her database information she kept to cross-reference with her clients."

"Did you bring a computer?"

"Yes, I did."

"Could I see the program?"

He hoped she wouldn't balk at showing him, and she didn't.

"Sure."

She loved to talk about, read about, and teach about this subject. She went up to her room for her laptop.

Adam looked around the little room. Catherine made this a great room to be in, he thought. The furniture was the kind he liked--roomy and covered with pale green corduroy, with a footstool ample enough to take all of a long leg. A large, scruffy, amiable dog, staring at him through the long hair that fell down over bushy eyebrows, occupied this one. He was absently scratching the dog's ears when she returned.

When Anne booted up, Reunion was on her desktop. When she opened it, she showed him the file set-up, pulling up her own name and the various ancestor configurations it could develop.

"Can you open your file list for me?"

"Sure."

She had only one file, her family.

"Who are you researching here?"

"My fifth great-grandmother who may have been a woman called Margaret or Marie Pewadjuonokwe. An aboriginal name obviously. She married a man called Charles Denis de la Ronde. One of my cousins found evidence Margaret was born and baptized here, so I came to follow it up."

She realized she was running on a bit and stopped talking, gazing thoughtfully at the detective.

He was smiling, taken with her enthusiasm. This woman is exactly what she seems, he thought.

"Is there anything of value found during research, like lost heirs, anything that would cause someone to steal computer files?"

"Not likely. Perhaps family secrets though. You know--melodrama stuff--ancestors who weren't quite the sort you wanted in your family or connections you thought were there that weren't; people of the wrong race, or color, or religion, or ethnicity. All that is possible I guess. Do you think her interest in genealogy got her killed?"

"I don't think anything yet, Dr. McPhail; I'm gathering information. Thank you for your help."

He stood up, shook her offered hand and went out to the kitchen to find Catherine.

"Would you like a something to drink?" she asked.

"No, thanks but if you know anything about Jennifer Smith, I'd like to hear it."

"Not a great deal but you're welcome to the gossip about what went on at the library."

Nancy and Jennifer got along, but only just. Two years before, the board chose her as Chief Librarian over long time employee Jennifer. Jennifer was not the type to hold a grudge but proceeded to make herself indispensable to Nancy, to regular library users, and to the many who made internet inquiries. She was a genius at research, especially searching the old records for traces of aboriginal ancestry, and for land claims. Catherine heard quite a few whispers that the board made a mistake.

As he drove back to the station through the pale light of an April afternoon, he noticed a lot of street-side activity for a Thursday. Little knots of people stood in front of stores and at street corners, eagerly talking. News travelled fast.

Chapter Four

Culver's Mills, population 10,000 more or less. Village green, white clapboard houses, a little industry, and a few professionals: it was mostly a service town for the surrounding agricultural community and for tourism. Quiet. Two prominent families: the Culvers whose family settled and named the place; and the Beauchamps - French Canadian likely, although old Mrs. Beauchamp insisted the ancestors arrived direct from France, and not with that the rag-tag bunch north of the border. Pride was a strange thing, Adam thought. Now he cared not at all about who his ancestors were or where they came from. He was who he was. Born in Vermont. Four years in college, two in the marines, ten years a policeman, all here in his home state.

He parked in front of the courthouse, which also housed the police station. Judge Wilmot should be free now, he thought. Re-elected fifteen times, fair, exacting and no pushover, he wasn't inclined to make a policeman's job more difficult.

Adam took the stairs two at a time up to the Judge's oak-paneled office. The Judge's secretary, Hazel, was an old friend of his. She looked like a hazel, he thought, with her brown hair and eyes and tanned skin.

"Hi, Adam," she said.

"Hi, Hazel. How's it going?"

He leaned over the desk to shake her hand and peck her cheek.

"Is he available now?"

"Waiting for you."

Judge Wilmot's office was like the man, unadorned. Simple shelving covered the walls, holding his library of law books. An open file folder, a telephone and a picture of his wife, occupied the desktop. Behind it sat the man himself, tall, slightly stooped with age now, but still with the commanding presence of the Marine Colonel he once was.

As Adam settled into a chair on the visitor's side of the desk, Judge Wilmot offered him a drink.

"No, thanks, Judge, I'm still working."

"What can I do for you?"

"I need a warrant to seize and examine the computer at the library. Someone downloaded files before or after Jennifer died. We need to try and recover them."

"And the problem?"

"Those files contain personal information on fifty-three different families who hired Jennifer to research their ancestry. I think we may find motive and maybe a pointer to the guy who did this."

The Judge thought for a moment. "Who would have access to these files?"

"Me, Brad Compton, our computer guy and maybe a genealogy expert."

"How are you going to find one of those?"

The Judge hadn't run across a genealogy expert before.

"The doctor who found the body could help. She knows a lot about the subject."

"Is she a suspect?"

The Judge's eyebrows went up as he looked at Adam across his half-glasses.

"No, I don't think so."

"Do you think she will be likely to keep things to herself?"

"Yes, I do, Judge. She seems sensible, and she's a doctor. Most of them can keep their mouths shut if they have to."

"Okay, here's your warrant, but you make sure she understands the limits."

"I will. Thanks, Judge."

Pete Graham paced at the reception desk. Waving the warrant, Adam called him, and they drove to the library. Young Dave, Pete's brother was still on guard.

"Anyone try to get in, Dave?"

"Miss Webb. She was some pissed when I wouldn't let her in."

"What did she want?"

Nancy would try.

"She said she needed some files for her work. I said nothing doing till you got here. I said I'd call her when you came. Is that okay?"

"Sure, go ahead."

They were stowing the library's one server and two workstations in the cruiser by the time Nancy Webb parked her late model Volvo wagon beside it. How much did librarians make? He drove a shaky 2008 Chev.

"Lieutenant, I hope you have a warrant."

She was way passed pissed off. Enraged was closer to it.

"Yes, ma'am."

He handed her the warrant and the receipt for the computers. She read every word, her face turning various shades of purple as she did.

"How am I supposed to run the library with no computers," she said.

"Same as you did before computers," he said as he got into the cruiser.

"That lady has something to hide," Pete said.

"Yeah, or else a very bad temper and a lot of self-importance. She's always been as miserable as sin. Is Brad ready to do the computer work?" he asked as he wheeled out of the parking spot.

"Yeah, but first he says he needs to know what to look for."

"He should find out if anything was deleted recently and if he can recover the files."

After the computers were set up at the station, Adam left, needing food, home and bed. Station house coffee wasn't enough. As he came around the corner of the square, he saw that the diner was still open.

He had been coming to Lil's since early high school when he was allowed to stay in town Friday evening. The red vinyl booths and chrome stools hadn't changed. The woman behind the counter was no longer Lil but Peg Watson, middle-aged, overworked, and curious. She listened, filed and connected all the gossip in town.

"Hey, Adam, how's it going?"

Peg smiled at Adam as she wiped the counter and set a napkin and cutlery in front of him.

"Not too bad, Peg. Could I have two of your famous chicken salad sandwiches on brown, toasted, fries, glass of milk?"

"Sure. How's the investigation coming along?"

Might as well ask was Peg's approach. Raised eyebrows lent a quizzical look on her thin, intelligent face with its dark brown eyes and long straight nose.

"Coming. What do you hear?"

He hoped the local network had come up with something about the dead woman that he hadn't heard. Genealogy was one thing but murder usually related to the life, loves, hates, or personality of the dead if it wasn't money.

"Most people don't understand it. She didn't seem to be the kind of person that would get herself murdered."

"Were you a friend of hers?"

"No, I only knew her from here and the library."

She passed him his food and went to serve some new arrivals. She still made the best chicken salad he had had anywhere, and he had tried it everywhere. He thought about what had she told him. Maybe it wasn't Jennifer Smith who was killed, but the assistant librarian, killed because of the job, not because of her personal life. That made less sense. Who kills an assistant librarian? What was she doing there hours before the library opened?

"When did you last see her?"

"Last night. She came in here about ten, had a coffee and some apple pie. She said she was on her way home, but she kept watching the clock. I figured she was meeting someone, but no one came. She left about 10:30pm, as I was closing."

So that's why Peg was upset—maybe the last person to see Jennifer alive, save for her killer.

"Was she annoyed?"

"No, a little...smug maybe, with a funny little half smile on her face. I have work to do, Adam."

"Yeah, let me have the bill."

His small house was only three blocks away. When he walked up to the side door, Sam, his cat called from the hall. She wound her soft black body around his legs. Give cats an A in seduction, he thought as he stroked her back. Her food bowl was empty. He fed the cat, called the station—no news —and signed out.

Chapter Five

The phone rang at 6:00am. Adam answered, covering his eyes against the early light.

"Yeah?"

"Pete. Another break-in at the library."

"What?"

Adam sat up in bed, wide-awake.

"About an hour ago, I think. Nothing gone. Maybe they were looking for the computers."

"Why? They took the files the first time."

"Who knows? Maybe they remembered we could recover the files."

"I'll be in."

Pete waited for him in front of the courthouse.

"What time did the alarm come in?"

Pete swung into the passenger seat and handed him a coffee.

"The alarm didn't sound. Sometimes those ladies forget to set it," he said, referring not only to the librarians but also to the legion of volunteers who helped in the library and the attached art gallery.

"Could be. Their alarm lets go if anyone tampers with it?"

"Supposed to, yeah."

"Who notified us?"

"Mrs. Majors, the dentist's wife was walking her dog in the park behind the library and saw the broken window. She called us as soon as she got home."

The street in front of the library was empty as they pulled into the parking lot. Adam still held keys, so they started at the back at the broken window and searched through the building. It was empty.

Glass had scattered over the cellar floor from the shattered window, but Adam didn't find any other damage. Perhaps the computers did hold the answer if that was what they were after.

By the time they finished, an agitated Nancy Webb arrived.

"What's happened here? I thought you were guarding the library?"

Enter talking, thought Adam. Might as well interview her now.

"I need to ask you a few questions."

A familiar panic come into her eyes. Meant nothing, even the innocent got that look.

"What sort of questions?"

She strode into her office and sat down behind her desk. Adam noticed a bunch of those objects that relieved stress: hanging balls to set in motion, worry beads, squeezable beanbags or something. He wondered why she felt the need for so many.

"When did you last see Jennifer alive?"

"Wednesday at lunchtime. She took the afternoon off as usual."

"Why did she take a half-day Wednesdays?"

A high note of resentment rose in her voice.

"I have no idea. She worked some Saturdays and took the time off instead of pay. Of course, I always worked Wednesday afternoon, no matter what I needed to do."

That's odd, he thought. Why make the arrangement if it didn't suit her? She was the boss.

"Why did you let her take the time off if you didn't want her to?"

"She was stubborn but useful. It would have taken a full confrontation and perhaps Board involvement to make her change. The Board wanted her to stay on—"

She turned and stared out the window.

"They valued her more than you?"

"I have a five-year contract," she said, swiveling to face him again.

"When was it up for renewal?"

"November."

"Will they renew?"

"Of course."

He remembered the gossip and wondered how likely renewal would be if Jennifer were alive.

"Where were you Thursday night?"

"You can't think I killed her?"

She gripped the edge of the desk so hard her knuckles blanched.

"I have to know, Nancy."

"I was at a Board meeting of the Historical Society until eleven, and then I went to a cafe with Brian Smith and Elizabeth Whalen. I went home about midnight. Brian dropped me at my door. You can ask him."

"Thanks, we will."

He glanced back as he left her. She sat, her eyes blank, her nervous fingers playing over a string of worry beads.

When Adam returned to the office, Brad was already working on the library computers.

Brad Compton was a junior officer, just out of Police College, after receiving a diploma from a technical college. He was, by all accounts, a computer whiz but you'd think he was a jock---no glasses, no stash of pens in his pocket. Tall and muscular, his crooked nose, broken in a high school football game, was the most prominent feature on his cheerful face.

Brad said he would take few hours to recover the files.

Adam thought it was time to learn a little more about the victim: how she lived, whom she knew, and how much money she had. He began at her house, taking Pete with him.

Mill Street was in the oldest part of town, running off the square. Fifteen was a cottage—story and a half, clapboard, some peeling paint but not too bad, new roof. Jennifer worked on the gardens last fall, ready for spring. She took care of her space.

A lane beside the house ran back to a garage behind. Where was her car? There were no car keys on the spare set he found in the desk.

"Did she have a car?" he asked Pete.

"Yes, a new Buick."

"See if it's in the garage."

Inside the front door, he paused again. The scene looked more desolate than yesterday, a little more abandoned. Funny how that always happened, as though the house got sadder the longer it stayed in a terrible mess.

The front door opened straight into the living room. The over-stuffed easy chairs were overturned and slashed. A sofa was the same. The antique chests and side tables weren't damaged although all the drawers were dumped on the floor. A Federal-style mirror hung above a white mantle over the fireplace. Good stuff, and expensive--what did librarians make?

Pete said the car was in the garage. Adam told him to search through Jennifer's papers for bank statements or financial records.

A narrow, steep staircase, closed on both sides, led upstairs. The first bedroom at the top had been hers. A slashed mattress hung off the four-poster bed. Adam examined an overturned nightstand and used a pen to open the lid of a jewelry case. The jewelry was still there, he saw with surprise. Not much but good stuff. The only other room was her office. Aside from the desk, it wore the stage set air of all spare rooms, decorated but not lived in, not as expensive.

Downstairs, he checked Pete's haul--a passbook from the Vermont Savings and Loan. The balance was $3,520 as of last Monday. No unusual withdrawals. A checkbook, same bank, different account—another damn warrant, he thought. He found a safety deposit box key in the drawer but no record of contents.

"I'll have to get the bank to unseal the box," Adam said.

Who had her lawyer been? A stack of business cards in a drawer suggested David Lepine. She seemed to have kept the cards of all the professionals she had used, from lawyer to computer salesperson. When they finished searching, he called Lepine, but he was out.

He needed more information about Jennifer's private life. Back to Lil's, he thought.

Over his usual, he asked Peg what more she knew about Jennifer. Not much, she said. Jennifer didn't gossip, at least not in the diner. She thought that the little theatre crowd would know more about her. Try David Mason, was her suggestion.

Mason's office was an easy walk across the square. It occupied a one-story brick house set back behind a picket fence and a small garden. The entrance to his office was the front door. Mason didn't live here. In the old days, Adam thought, patients used the second door off the porch. The waiting room was full. Could he come back, the secretary asked.

"We have a very busy office today," she said, her eyes focused on her computer screen.

Adam insisted, and she ushered him into the presence.

Mason was the only chiropractor in town, tall and thin, a pencil line of a moustache above equally-thin lips. Not an easy smiler, at least not today.

"What can I tell you about Jennifer, Detective?" he asked as he stood safely behind his desk.

"Can we sit down?" said Adam, sitting. The guy needed to understand that this might take some time, busy office or not. "How well did you know her?"

Mason tapped a pencil on the computer keyboard on his desk.

"Not too well. She wasn't a patient. She directed in the little theater; I acted."

Adam noted that Mason was impatient, annoyed and perhaps nervous. Was there something behind the spare statements?

"How long have you been involved?"

"What can you mean?"

"I mean in the little theatre."

"Oh, about ten years."

"Was Jennifer always in the theatre?"

"Yes, she was one of the founders and told you so at every available opportunity. That was why she directed, even though others would have enjoyed it and done a better job."

Everybody didn't like Jennifer, Adam thought.

"How did the others feel about her? Did she have any friends or was one group for her, one against?"

Mason drew himself up sharply.

"How can this possibly help you? None of these people are vicious enough to crack her skull. Many of them are my patients and I can't talk to you about them."

The thin lips pursed as he withdrew inside his professional shell.

"Tell me who they are, Dave."

"I can give you the membership list."

"Do you have it here?"

"Yes, I keep most of my theatre business papers here because I'm the president this year. The cast is small. We are doing Six Characters in Search of an Author, so there were only about fifteen involved altogether."

Adam read Erin Maxell's name on the roster.

"Fine. I may have to talk to you again," Adam said as he left the office.

Chapter Six

A row of police cars lined up behind the library. Still investigating the scene, Anne thought. She didn't feel quite as weak at the knees as she had after the finding the body when she climbed the stairs to the reference library. While she researched her own family, she hoped to find a little information about the young French woman of the diary.

The next step would be to look at the census data. She knew the library held copies of local records on microfilm as well as some important early historical documents. Her own membership in Ancestry.com, an Internet genealogy company, would be helpful as well.

The reference library opened off the same hallway as the art gallery. She waved to Ada Warren and called good morning to her.

The librarian gave her the diary and showed her the library's collection of microfilmed data. Two hours later, Anne looked up in surprise as the students, and older researchers left en mass. Lunchtime. A good time to work, she thought, as she took one of the vacated microfilm readers.

She slotted the tape under the wheels and the glass plate of the viewer. Nice, she thought. Brand new, with the automatic printer feature that helped record keeping. She scrolled through the census, one local district at a time.

Sometimes luck was with her and her family showed up early. Not this time but at the end of the census reel, she found them--Margaret and her children. No man. Either she was widowed or abandoned, or he was travelling. The children came at odd intervals, not the one to two years natural spacing would have produced if the man were around all the time. Two girls and three boys. The early census didn't identify people by name, just sex, age group and race. Only the head of the household was named. The local churches would have some information, she hoped.

Anne walked in the bright sunshine across the square to Lil's for lunch. The old stone building occupied one corner of the square and David St. Up three stairs, through a heavy door and into a wave of sound: high-pitched voices of teenage girls; a low growl from a table of businessmen; excited chatter from another of elderly ladies. Anne found a stool at the counter.

"What would you like today?" asked the pleasant-faced server as she poured her a coffee.

"Bacon, lettuce and tomato, salad, and a Diet Coke, please," said Anne, reading from the menu chalked on a board above the pass-through to the kitchen.

"Sure. Brown toast?"

"Please."

She sipped her coffee, excellent as usual in the States, while she listened to the conversations that drifted her way.

"Did you hear about the library?"

"The murder, you mean?"

"No, this morning. Someone broke in again."

"Huh. What would anybody steal from the library?"

"Who knows?"

So that's why all the police this morning. What sort of evidence could the murderer have left behind? She hadn't seen much.

A pair of uniformed policemen sat down on the stools next to her.

"What did Davidson find this morning?"

"Nothing missing as far as they could tell."

Anne paid her bill and walked back through the park and down the street to the library. This afternoon she had decided to search the newspaper archive for the ten years between the censuses of 1800 and 1810.

The Bon Chance Crier, later the Culver's Mills Enterprise had been founded in 1798 and continuously published to this day, the librarian told her proudly.

She was happy microfilm existed for the early years. Old newspapers caused her allergies to flare. The librarian took reels for the early years from a file drawer.

By four o'clock she had about given up for the day when a small announcement caught her eye: a wedding between Marie-Angelique de la Ronde and Michel Beauchamp.

I wonder if the Beauchamp family has this piece of information and if they would be happy to know it, she mused. Maybe Catherine would have some idea.

She printed a copy of the page and left for the day, looking forward to a bath and a pleasant dinner. She and Catherine seemed to have connected. She hoped they would become good friends.

Chapter Seven

Adam left the courthouse that bounded the north side of the square. The white-painted Methodist church dominated the south end with rows of houses, stores and offices in between. The whole thing was picture post-card Vermont.

Two antique stores, one promising *decorating hints*, a doctor's office, two lawyers and the chiropractor filled the east side of the square. Erin Maxwell's antique store took up the corner.

Its window held a cradle, two barley-twist candlesticks, an occasional table and a framed old-Yankee portrait, no decorating hints. The interior was definitely antique store, not junk shop. No tables piled with color-coordinated glassware here, but tidy collections of furniture accompanied by all the appropriate accessories. A row of hanging lamps lit the shop. Erin sat with a customer at the back, at the oval dining table that doubled as a desk.

Erin was in her early thirties, not tall, and slender. Her sweater, skirt, and pendant combination was just right for the store. He knew that appearances were a little off. He met her when she reported the abuse of a child who attended a swimming class she taught. During the investigation, she shared some of her own past.

She was born in Burlington to a mother who had married her trucker boyfriend right out of high school. She was the youngest of their five children, born long after any pretense of love and or happiness had gone from the relationship. Bob Maxwell was absent, most of the time and hard drinking, belligerent and abusive when he came home. Although his favorite, from a young age his treatment of her mother angered her. She left to go to school paid for with scholarships and after-school jobs, as soon as she was seventeen. She took a degree in fine arts. She loved antiques, so a legacy from an aunt went straight into setting up in Culver's Mills.

"Hi. Can I have a few minutes?" Adam said as the customer left.

"Sure," she said as she put the Closed, Back in 15 sign in the window. "Come in for tea."

The back room of the shop served as office, kitchen and storage. The china was Royal Worcester, the teapot Spode, little elegant touches in the crowded room.

"Do you know that Jennifer Smith was killed?" he asked.

"Yes, I heard it on the radio this morning."

Her mobile face drooped and lost color. Her dark brown eyes and brown hair deepened her pallor.

"Did you know her well from theatre?"

"Yes, but also from the library. She was helpful whenever I was researching furniture or a piece of glass or china. She loved research—all kinds, but especially genealogy. At the theater, she was different, rougher, not as kind. I wasn't going to go back after this play."

"That's too bad," he said.

"Yes, but it wasn't as bad for me as for the actors. She was cruel to some of them. I'm only a prompter and stage manager. She was awful to Elizabeth Baker and Cliff Madison, worse this year than last. If she could make them look ridiculous, she did. There was a scene last Tuesday. They both looked daggers at her. Oh, what an expression. I really don't like talking about this."

She bit on her knuckles, a child-like trait he found endearing.

"Erin, I have to ask about her, if I'm going to be able to find her killer. Murder is ugly. It lets loose all kinds of secrets and hates. I have to sort it out."

He took her hand, a gesture he hadn't made before. She squeezed his hand and took it away to pour the tea.

She peered at him over her dainty china cup and said, "Stan Davis was involved with her, I think."

"I don't think I know him."

He gingerly lifted the delicate cup. She loved tea, so he drank tea with her.

"He comes from Greenbank. He's a lawyer over there."

Greenbank was another small town about 30 miles away.

"Yeah, now I remember him—a short, stocky guy with red hair who works out and runs."

"That's him. I saw them together in a restaurant in Burlington. They seemed close."

She poured a little more tea.

"Like lovers? Or conspirators?"

"It would look the same from across the room, wouldn't it?"

"I suppose so."

He stood up to go and asked if she would like to go out to dinner with him."

"Sure, but not until next week."

"Tuesday?"

"Good."

"I'll call you."

Adam left the shop. Every stop, another few more people he had to interview. He called Pete to talk to the angry actors while he drove the thirty miles to Greenbank unless the guy was in court.

He got the number of the law office from dispatch and called Davis and O'Connor. The lawyer was at the courthouse, so he headed back to the station and his next witness. What did involved mean anyway--in business, in love, in politics?

He found Davis outside courtroom A. The oak benches lining the narrow hallway jostled together everyone attending court: young women and their babies, waiting for family court with their protection workers; bikers in metal studded leather jackets; sullen teenagers slouching beside taut-faced parents.

A door off the entrance to the courtroom opened into a windowless room for duty counsel. He found Davis there, feet up on a battered table, rapidly reviewing a brief.

"Can you spare me a few minutes, Mr. Davis?"

"Court in two minutes," he said, eyes still on the page.

He looked up.

"I'll be done in two hours."

"I'll be back."

Adam could be abrupt, too.

The office was empty except for Brad and his computer. He poured himself one of his too many coffees of the day and came around the desk to peer over Brad's shoulder.

"Any luck?"

"I've recovered most of the files I think."

Brad's voice was proud. Apparently, it had been no mean feat.

"Good job."

The younger man flushed at the praise. He had started printing hard copies, he said, and would likely be finished by the end of the shift.

"He was researching the Beauchamps."

The rich always stood out on any list.

"Who was the client?"

"I'm not sure that I got that entire file though. I thought they came from France, way back, but this says the ancestors were from Quebec."

Brad didn't realize that this could be a disaster for the stiff-necked Beauchamp clan. Disaster enough to murder? More interviews, his favorite kind, with people who thought they were too rich and too important to talk to him.

"Did you find anything else interesting?"

"Not locally interesting. Most of the files are about out-of-town families."

"Will you separate the copies into local, state, USA, and out of country?"

"Sure, no problem, sir."

As he passed through the office, he saw his chief, Jim Naismith at his desk. Jim Naismith had been chief of police here for twenty years, on the force for forty. He, Adam and a few others were all the police they needed for the town. The chief was a burly, strong-looking sixty years old, grizzled with dark grey eyes and a round face.

"How's it going? Making any progress?"

"Not too much. I haven't got any witness to Jennifer arriving at the library. I don't even have a time of death yet."

"I'll be in Burlington for a meeting today. You can hold the fort?"

"Sure."

Adam called down to the Medical Examiner's office.

"Kim," he asked the secretary, "has Al finished the report for me yet?"

"I'm typing it now. Poor lady. Why did it happen?"

"Don't know yet. Do you have a time of death?"

"He says about midnight, give or take two hours."

"So ten to two the night before."

"Yes, if you find him, we think we have tissue under the fingernails for DNA."

"If I find him."

Adam couldn't place Jennifer at the library, much less her killer. He did know that she had been alive at 10:30pm. Someone must have seen her, although most citizens of Culver's Mills were on their way to bed then. He paused after hanging up the phone. There had been bowling that night. Someone may have passed the library.

Chapter Eight

Culver's Mills Bowling Lanes occupied a long, low building on a nondescript side street behind a beauty salon. Gliding semipro players occupied all the lanes when Adam walked in. Tim Hunter, a grin splitting his round face, reached across the counter to shake his hand.

"Good to see you, Adam."

"You too, Tim. Is there someplace where I could talk to you?"

"Sure, come into my office."

Adam walked around the counter and into a cubbyhole of a room behind the counter. Two chairs and a filing cabinet, its top covered with bowling trophies, just about filled the space. He moved files off a chair before he sat.

"What's up?" Tim asked.

They had gone to high school together, playing on the same football team.

"I need information about Wednesday night's bowlers. Can you tell me who was here and who left last?" said Adam, settling back into his chair.

"Sure. Wednesdays are the seniors. They break up a little early. Let me grab the game list."

He pulled a paper off a clipboard hanging by the door.

"Who left last?"

"Ada Warren and Maude Albert. Ada's the organizer, so she wants to make sure everyone has a drive and so on. They left about ten thirty, quarter of eleven."

"Thanks, Tim."

"Looking for witnesses?"

"Something like that."

He shook Tim's hand again and walked out.

Adam drove to Chester Warren's house, or rather his widow's since Chester had died last year. Ada was a trim and active seventy-five-year-old, formerly a schoolteacher, now an artist, local historian and demon bowler. The trick was to find her at home. He rang the bell and heard the high-pitched barking of her fierce little Lhasa Apso terrier.

"Quiet, Tom."

"Why, hello, Adam."

She had taught him in high school twenty years before.

"Hello, Ada. Could I have a few minutes of your time? I'd like to ask you a couple of questions about your bowling night."

He extended a hand as he passed into the tiny foyer.

"My bowling night. Of course, the night Jennifer died. Is this about her? Please sit down."

Ada took him into her living room and patted a comfortable recliner.

"Yes, it does. What time did you leave the bowling alley?" he asked.

"About ten thirty."

As usual, Ada chose a firm, straight-backed chair. Easier on old bones, she always said.

"When you drove home, did you pass the library, or see anything unusual?"

"I passed the library. I didn't notice Jennifer or anyone sneaking around. A car parked near the library near the library had the lights off but I someone sat in it. Then I thought, just a couple necking, except I can't say I saw two heads. A grey car, I think, although it could have been pale blue, a sedan. American. I think the license started with vx."

"Ada, you're still my favorite teacher. Was anyone with you?"

"Yes, Maude Albert, but she concentrates when she's driving."

He laughed. Tiny Maude Albert in her ancient, immense Cadillac was well known. She lived next door to Mrs. Warren, so he paid her a visit. She couldn't recall any details of the car.

On his way back to the office, he called in his information on the vehicle Mrs. Warren saw and asked for the record on Davis's car. The lawyer was walking down the courthouse steps towards the red Camaro as Adam parked.

"Leaving, Mr. Davis? We had an appointment."

"Just stowing my briefcase, detective. Do you want to get a drink? I've been talking for two hours."

Davis was casual and affable, cooperative with nothing to hide.

"We better have it in the station."

Adam followed the lawyer to the office, stopping to fill their cups on the way.

"Mr. Davis, my information is you knew the murder victim, Jennifer Smith."

Adam came to the point abruptly as they sat down in the office.

"Yes, I did," he said.

"How well?"

"We were friends."

"My information is that you had dinner with her in Burlington, looking quite close. Are you married, Mr. Davis?"

"That's an offensive way to ask a question. No, I am not married. Divorced. And we weren't that close. She asked my advice about her job."

Davis sat back in his chair, folding his arms across his chest.

"What about her job?"

"She was thinking about setting up on her own as a genealogy consultant."

"A genealogy consultant."

Adam was grateful he now knew what that was.

"Does that mean she would give up the library?"

"That was the problem. The library board doesn't allow moonlighting. Jennifer had many clients, but the library board considered they were the library's, not hers. The fees went into the general revenue. If she left, they wouldn't let her take any of her information databases or files out of the library."

Adam thought for a moment. Did Jennifer copy those files herself? If so, where were they?

"Did she give you any computer disks to keep for her, counselor?"

"No, detective, she did not. Remember I was her friend, not her lawyer."

"What was her decision?"

"She didn't make one. At least, she hadn't the last time I talked to her. But she was excited about some research she had found. She didn't want to tell me that day. We were supposed to have dinner tonight."

Adam thought Davis was genuinely saddened at the memory.

"I guess that's all then, Mr. Davis. If you think of anything else, you let me know."

"I'll do that."

The lawyer marched out of the office, brushing past Brad who knocked, entered the office, and triumphantly handed him a stack of paper.

"What's all this?"

"The hard copies from Jennifer's files. I divided them. The three on top, the Beauchamps, the Culvers and Doctor McPhail, are local. I put her in because she is here now. There were ten in state, and the rest are from out of the state or out of the country. Usually, there is only an inquiry from those. She completed the families in state. The last activity on most of them was last year. She was working on a file called Templeton from Burlington, and the three locals."

"Thanks. Leave them with me."

"Okay. It sure is hard stuff to follow," Brad said.

Adam took up the top file, Dr. McPhail's. He looked through several pages, which seemed to build up layer upon layer of ancestors, with herself as the first contact, all the way back to many greats grandmother Margaret. The notes on the family tree followed bits of information about everything from marriages to education, from military service to immigration and naturalization. If there were any secrets worth killing for he couldn't find them, but he also wasn't sure what to look for. He decided to pay the doctor another visit.

A familiar figure slouched over the receptionist's desk. The press had arrived. Ted Atkins, forty years old, paunchy, a sad sack of a face too old for his years, followed the crime and sports beats for the local paper. Adam knew a family tragedy had brought him to Culver's but not what had kept him here, year after year. His writing stood out from the village news columns and clergy reports that filled the pages of the weekly.

"Adam, open season on librarians, is it? Anything you can give me?"

"I haven't had time to do a press release."

"Name of deceased, time of death, how did she die? A few crumbs. We go to press in an hour."

"Okay. Here's all you can have for now. Jennifer Smith, the assistant librarian, found dead at the library, after opening time, by a patron of the library. She was a victim of blunt force trauma. Perpetrator unknown at this time. The investigation is continuing."

"Sexual assault?"

"No, and don't you even imply it, Ted."

"Okay, okay. What else? Robbery?"

"Nothing else today. Catch me later."

"But."

"Later."

Adam raced out the door and through the court foyer before Ted asked another question.

~

Anne knelt beside the flower bed that bordered the porch of the bed and breakfast.

"Helping out are you, Dr. McPhail?" he asked as he walked up to her.

"I think I love gardening more than genealogy."

Anne looked happy and grubby in her Tilley hat, dark glasses and a mud-stained t-shirt that proclaimed *I like to play in the dirt*. "Are you here to talk to me again?"

"Yes, ma'am. I wonder if you would help with Jennifer's genealogy files?"

"Certainly. If I can help, I will but should I be seeing private files?"

"I have a warrant, and you are my consultant. Can we sit awhile?"

He indicated the two slatted wooden chairs on the porch.

"This one is yours," he said, handing it to her."

"Oh, great. I wonder if Jennifer found anything."

She eagerly scanned the file.

"She found a record of a baptismal certificate. Margaret was born and christened here. My cousin was right. Now I have to see if she was married here as well. Jennifer didn't do that yet. I wonder why she did so much ahead of time? I told her I would do the scut work myself."

Anne stopped talking, aghast at her own enthusiasm over the dead woman's work.

"Oh, I'm sorry. I shouldn't go on and on about this."

"No problem, doc. Try the next file."

He gave her the Culver file.

"Culver—founding fathers are they?"

"Yes, they sure are."

"Jennifer began with someone called David Culver and went back through several generations. The name changes about 1800 to Calvert. French I would think, perhaps originally de Colvere but not common among the old Quebec names."

"How do you know?"

"There are only a few original names, most of them still common in Quebec. Jennifer's notes indicate the ancestor came over with Lafayette. The family lived here since the early 1800's when the original Culver, a grandson of the one who immigrated, opened the mill. The weddings took place in Burlington or Montreal in the early years, later in New York. No local ones. I wonder about that."

"Why?"

"The family was large, but none of the children married into local families, not even the other French family, the Beauchamps."

"How do you know about the Beauchamps?"

"I ran across some references at the library."

"Their file is next, but my computer guy says he couldn't recover it all."

"The initial contact was a woman called Nicole Bouchard. She seems to be a cousin of your local family. The letter in the file says she lives in Montreal and is looking for her grandmother's family. The information is sketchy. Either Jennifer wasn't thorough, or much of this is gone, including the notes to all the individuals.

"Could you redo the research?"

"I don't know. I would need access to all of Jennifer's databases and reference material. Even then I might miss the important fact."

She raised her eyebrows at the detective.

"What important fact?"

"The one that got Jennifer killed, Adam."

If she was going to be a colleague she was going to call him by his first name.

"A big assumption."

"Yes, but it does seem logical, especially when someone broke into the library again."

"How do you know that?"

"Diner at lunchtime."

"Sure, better than the front page. How long did you plan to be here?"

"I'm fairly free. I inherited some money last year and decided to retire from my practice. I don't have any close family, and a friend is looking after my cat so I can stay here as long as I want to. Within reason," she said with a faint smile.

"Can you start today?"

"No, tomorrow morning. I have some plans for today".

"Please keep it to yourself. I don't want you in any danger."

"I will," she said a little unsteadily.

Personal danger didn't occur to her when she agreed. She wasn't very brave. Not really brave, she thought. Then she resumed her gardening. Attacking weeds always had a calming effect on her.

It was close to 7:00pm when Adam got back to the station. Pete lowered the window of his new truck.

"Hey, Pete. Nice looking vehicle. How did your interviews go?"

"Thanks. I picked it up last weekend," Pete said as he ran his hand lovingly over the steering wheel. "I put the report on your desk. They were mad as hell at Jennifer, but their alibis for the time period are solid. The Madisons spent the night in the emergency room with a sick baby, and the Bakers left at 5:00pm that day for an overnight in Burlington. She had a doctor's appointment the next morning. They checked into a hotel at eight. Room service at nine. Movie ordered at 10:00pm and wake-up call at 7:00am. Maybe one of them sneaked out, but the desk clerk doesn't think so."

"Why are they so mad?"

"It was like Ms. Maxwell told you. She stuck it to them good, every rehearsal. They said she changed quite a bit over the last six months. Mean."

"Thanks. See you in the morning'

Pete drove off as Adam ran up the steps of the courthouse. He still needed a warrant for Jennifer's safety box and bank accounts. Fortunately, the judge was free and agreeable. He would execute the warrants tomorrow.

Chapter Nine

Lil's diner was packed when Anne dropped in for coffee before going to the police station. Memories of her own teenage Friday nights at Haramis's restaurant flooded back as she smelled the French fries and listened to the high-pitched, excited chatter of the teenage girls. French fries for breakfast. It had been a long time.

A short red-haired man in a business suit standing at the cash turned as Dougal, one of the twins called to her, "I hear you're going to help Lieutenant Davidson solve the murder, Dr. McPhail."

"Shush, Dougal."

His freckled face fell.

"Gee, I'm sorry, Dr. McPhail. I didn't know it was a secret."

"That's all right. It isn't really, but it's better not to talk about it."

Anne didn't notice the alert look that came into the eyes of the sad-faced man sitting next to her at the counter or know that he watched her as she walked across to the courthouse. She stopped to read the message on the statue in the park, rubbing its toe for luck before she walked on. Chuck LaPlante, Dougal's brother, called to her as she reached the courthouse steps.

"Hey, Dr. McPhail, are you a giving a statement?"

"Not today, Chuck."

A black SUV, sitting at the curb with the window down, drove in behind the courthouse. Anne's car, conspicuous with its Ontario plates, was the only one in visitor parking. A few minutes later the other car drove off.

Anne walked into the police section of the courthouse, expecting a high counter with a grizzled sergeant to demand gruffly what she wanted. However, the door opened straight into the expansive common office. A middle-aged, comfortable-looking woman in a navy sweater directed her to a young man seated at a grey, steel desk. He grinned a friendly greeting to her.

"Hi," he said, "I'm Brad Compton, Dr. McPhail. Can I get you some coffee?"

Anne smiled back at him as she held up her take-out cup. "Brought my own."

"Did you already hear about ours?"

Brad showed her the information he had on the databases in the computer as well as Jennifer's program. Anne was impressed with the amount of information Jennifer accumulated. She also asked Brad to go online so they could access information in the Church of Latter Day Saints database and others. She began the slow task of reconstructing the Beauchamp family tree.

She looked up from her work when Adam stopped at her desk.

"Thanks for coming in, Anne. How's it going?"

"Not too bad. There are a lot of years to cover. Brad helped me get the databases I needed."

"Okay. Ask if you need anything more."

He picked up his warrants and called Darlene Utronski to tell her what they were going to do. She asked him to speak to Dave Lepine, her sister's lawyer.

Lepine and Wagger, Law Offices were diagonal across the square from the courthouse, and beside the bank. Adam had called David Lepine the day before and arranged to meet him at the bank when he had acknowledged being Jennifer's lawyer.

"Morning, Davidson."

One of those guys who insist on calling you by your last name, he was medium height, jaw pushed in, too many teeth, bad acne scars, big ears. Good in court, Adam thought—pugnacious.

"Morning. I have the order to open her accounts and her safety deposit box. Mr. Canal said he would meet us here."

Adam handed over the papers for inspection. As he did so, the bank manager pulled up in his Volvo. Dark green, Adam noticed and not new.

"Morning, all."

Cheerful for a banker, he led the way into the bank, past the row of curious tellers behind their high counter, to the massive, steel door of the vault. The door itself was open, but the barred gate was locked. Behind it was a small room lined with safety deposit boxes and a tall counter, with a single small table filling the center of the room.

After the usually complicated formalities with keys, and signature cards the manager removed Jennifer's box. She rented the largest of the three models. The manager used the key that Adam handed him to open it, but turned it to face the lawyer and the detective as he placed it on the table. At the looks on their faces, he came around the table to see for himself.

Neat stacks of currency, all in denominations of five hundred or one thousand dollar bills, as well as a jewel case, filled the box. The banker's hand went out to touch the money when Adam stopped him.

"It needs to be counted."

"We can put it through the machine. Come into my office, and I'll see what else I can find out on the computer."

While one of the clerks counted the money, Mr. Canal accessed Jennifer's accounts. Besides the ones Adam had found, she also had an investment account containing $100,000. The money in the box totaled another $100,000. The deposits into her savings had included regular cash deposits of $8,000 weekly at a time, just under the $10,000 limit that would have drawn the bank's attention and that of the IRS. The jewel case contained an unset diamond and some small antique pieces.

There was no helpful paper trail, just week after week of steady cash deposits, spread out among several different accounts, mostly made at the Burlington branch of the bank. Blackmail, Adam wondered, or some other illicit enterprise? He thought it was time to interview Stan Davis again.

"Do you have any ideas about this, Mr. Lepine?"

Adam's tone was blunt and far from affable.

"Hell, no. I even gave her a break on fees because I thought librarians weren't well paid."

The lawyer was as astonished as the bank manager.

Adam called Pete to come with evidence bags, and together they took the money back to the station and stored it securely in the evidence room.

"What next, boss?" Pete asked as they wolfed down take-out hamburgers and fries at their desks.

"Time to interview the Culvers. They were on Jennifer's local list."

"You or me?"

"I'll go. You drive to Burlington and see Darlene Utronski. Check out her lifestyle. See if Jennifer was sharing the wealth. I want a report on Nancy Webb, too. Maybe all that stuff between them was just show."

"Ted Atkins called. Wanted to know how a Canadian doctor came to be "helping you with your inquiries". Said it with a British accent. That some kind of joke?"

"Search me. I gave Atkins all he needs to know for now."

Adam stopped by to talk to Anne and warn her about the reporter, but she'd gone to have lunch with Catherine at a small inn a few miles from town.

The Culver home was off the main square and on the river. Lawns reaching to the river bank, and very extensive gardens formed a park-like setting. The house itself was white clapboard, well cared for, with green shutters. A question--were there still servants--was answered when a large but tidy woman in a simple grey dress opened the door.

"Good morning, I'm Lieutenant Davidson of the Culver's Mills police," he said as he showed her his identification. "Could I see Mrs. Culver, please?"

"Certainly, sir."

The housekeeper turned to leave, but he called her back.

"Could you tell me who you are?"

"Beatrice Ames. I'm the housekeeper here."

She seemed nervous, careworn hands twisting as she spoke. The back of one was bandaged. The hands of a woman who worked for a living, he thought.

"Thank you."

He waited in the hall as she went in search of one of the Culvers.

The accumulated possessions of generations of the Culvers, all cared for, all in good taste, were becoming just a little threadbare. No decorator's touch here.

A dark, wiry young man of about thirty, bounded down the stairs.

"David Culver, Lieutenant Davidson. Mrs. Ames said you wanted a word with me."

He had a very careful accent, a bit English, Adam thought.

"Yes, I'm investigating Jennifer Smith's death. I understand you or your family employed her to do some digging into your family's past."

"Indeed. How do you know that, Detective?"

The patrician accent was becoming annoyed.

"Computer files, Mr. Culver. We have a warrant to look at Jennifer's genealogy files."

"That includes very private information."

He drew back his head. Just like a turtle, Adam thought, or a buzzard.

"We know that. Only information relevant to our investigation will be used. Is there anything in particular that you are worried about?"

"Of course not." Culver said, his color rising and getting a panicked look in his eyes.

As the two men faced each other in the hall, an elderly lady, striking in a high-necked, well-cut dress of some sort of red wool walked carefully down the stairs. She must have been beautiful when she was young, Adam thought, and she still had a proud carriage.

"David, what are you yelling about?"

He had only raised his voice, but maybe that passed for a shout in this house.

"Grandmother, this policeman is here about the work Jennifer did for us. They are looking at the files," he said in a desperate tone.

"What are you so concerned about?"

"But the history—"

"Please leave us."

Brushing aside his protests she waited until he had stalked down the hall and disappeared, then turned to Adam.

"Mister?"

"Davidson."

"Please come with me, Mr. Davidson."

She took him into a small study. Upright wingback chairs, a cherry wood desk, framed watercolor of a pointer above the fireplace: a room that Adam would have liked to spend time in.

"Mr. Davidson, my grandson is too precipitous. He also has an exaggerated idea of the consequences of some scandal present in a family's history."

Her stiff posture echoed her stern words.

"What was Jennifer doing for you, Mrs. Culver?"

"Some years ago, a letter was found in one of the boxes in the attics here that suggested a disgraceful episode in my husband's great-grandfather's family. We hired Jennifer to prove or disprove the allegation."

45

"I'll need to know what effect the allegation would have today," he said.

He was pushing a little. If the information didn't show in the files he had a warrant for, he wasn't sure he could insist on an answer.

"The allegation was that the great-grandfather had had a liaison with a servant in his home, an Irish girl, producing a child, and therefore a second and related Culver line in this community."

Her pale cheeks colored a vivid pink.

"What effect would that have on the finances of this family?"

His first rule—follow the money.

"None at all. The laws until recently favored legitimate over illegitimate children. Some members of my family, perhaps the younger ones, take this very seriously indeed, but I assure you, Mr. Davidson, not enough to kill the messenger. Jennifer hadn't been able to find any evidence when last she reported to me."

Mrs. Culver stood up, apparently thinking that the interview was over.

Adam, standing, asked, "Which members of your family took this seriously, Mrs. Culver?"

Before she could answer, David and a young woman Adam recognized as David's sister Natalie entered the room. Natalie had her grandmother's fine bones and posture, but the pride had turned to arrogance.

"We did, Detective."

"Then perhaps you could tell me where you were Wednesday evening and early Thursday morning?"

"I don't think we have to," said David.

"No, but if you don't tell me I will be investigating you," Adam told him.

"For heaven's sake, David. We took Grandmother to Burlington to a concert. We had dinner with friends. We got back at one-thirty and went to bed."

"May I have their names please?"

"Yes."

Natalie scribbled hastily at the desk.

"Now, please go," she said, as she thrust the paper at him.

As he left, he saw the quiet housekeeper watching him from the top of the stairs.

Chapter Ten

The blued-steel look of snow coming colored the sky to the northwest. Not unusual for early April in Vermont, but not welcome either. The first flakes were hitting the windshield as Adam reached the courthouse. He called Pete in Burlington to check on the Culvers' alibis, although a 1:30am return did not let them out entirely.

The office/squad room was empty except for Brad and his computer. No sign of Anne. Seemed to be a long lunch, but he wasn't paying her.

"Any luck, Brad?"

"I'm working backwards on the Culvers. Dr. McPhail said this file was complete back a few generations but had gaps at the beginning."

"When did she say she would be back?"

"About 2:00pm. What time is it now, boss?"

"1:30pm. Get some lunch."

Adam took his messages from the front desk. Atkins called again, and Mrs. Ames called. Who was Mrs. Ames? Oh, yeah, the Culver housekeeper. He thought she had something to say. Call after 6, the message read. He had time to track Davis, Jennifer's lawyer friend, to ask about her unexpected income. Greenbank was a few miles away, and a phone call to his office went unanswered, so Adam decided to leave the interview until later and write reports.

Two hours later, he leaned back from the desk. No clear path anywhere. He looked out at Brad and his computer—no Anne. The weather had settled in, the slow, steady, Vermont snowfall that piled up fast. She's Canadian, he thought. She knows how to drive in snow.

The squad room door opened. Atkins again.

"Adam, I hear we're importing medical talent to work on our homicides. Old Doc Patterson not good enough anymore?"

"Come in, Ted. Sit down for a minute."

Adam decided to try and protect Anne by giving Ted a little more information.

"Sure, coffee on?"

"Help yourself."

When Ted came back with his mug, Adam said, "You have your what, where, and whatever those other w words you work to are."

"Why, and how it was done and who did it are still missing. What's this McPhail woman got to do with it? She found the body. Is she a suspect? And where did Jennifer get all the money?"

"Dr. McPhail is helping us and, no, she is not a suspect."

"Have you found the murder weapon?"

"No murder weapon has been found."

"Motive?"

"None established at this time. That's all I have for you."

"And little it is."

At that, the reporter stood up and ambled out of the office.

Where did the reporter get the information about Jennifer's money? Could have come from the bank, he supposed, although bankers were a tight-lipped lot. Even bankers talked to their wives.

Across the square, the doorbell tinkled in Erin's shop. She was surprised to see the tall figure of Beatrice Ames walk through towards her. Beatrice had only been in the shop once before, to buy a gift for her mother.

"Good afternoon, Miss Maxwell."

"Good afternoon, Mrs. Ames. What can I help you with today?"

How nervous she is Erin thought, watching the large hands twisting as the older lady spoke.

"Oh, dear. You might be offended if I ask you."

"Of course, I won't be offended. Ask away."

"It's that young man, Lieutenant Davidson."

She stopped and peered anxiously at Erin.

"You know him, don't you?"

"Yes, I do?"

"Is he a kind man?"

"Kind? Yes, he's kind and understanding. Do you need to talk to him?"

Beatrice continued wringing her hands. She shook her large head, as though to clear it and paused a long minute before answering.

"Yes, I do, but I must go."

She turned and was out the door before a surprised Erin could speak.

She'd tell Adam, Erin thought, but before she picked up the phone another customer came in, and she put off calling.

Chapter Eleven

From his office, Adam stared out at the worsening storm. Blowing snow filled the parking lot and hid the row of houses along the square.

Brad reported he hadn't heard from Anne, and neither had Catherine LaPlante. The women finished lunch at 1:30pm and left separately. Anne headed back to the station while Catherine intended to visit an elderly friend who lived in a local nursing home.

Catherine changed her mind with the snow starting and went home instead. She wasn't far ahead of Anne, she thought.

Adam pulled Brad from the computer and took the keys for the four by four from the desk and drove out to the inn.

Anne cast a worried eye on the dark clouds before she left the parking lot and hoped she'd get back to Culver's Mills before the storm.

The inn sat at the top of a paved lane that wound up a long, winding hill. Halfway down the hill, the visibility dropped. The rear wheels skidded slightly as she went around a curve. Slower, she told herself. The road couldn't be more than a kilometer, she thought.

The snow fell faster, and the wind picked up. Faint tracks of a vehicle that went down ahead of her were all that marked the road. The edges blurred into the fields and forest beyond. Thick snow covered the red stop sign, but it was visible enough to tell her where the lane ended and the highway began.

She sat for a moment and breathed, loosening her grip on the steering wheel. The choice was either forward or turn around and go back up the hill. A left-hand turn took her onto the highway.

A Jeep or something like it loomed in her rearview mirror. Why did he have to be so close, she thought, angry at having another thing to worry about. She couldn't go any faster. The grill of the larger vehicle filled her mirror.

"I can't go any faster," she spoke aloud, frantically flashing her lights, trying to get him to back off.

As the cars rounded a curve, the Jeep pulled past, scraping the side of the vehicle, nudging her onto the shoulder. Anne lost control, as the deepening snow pulled the car's wheels. The car plunged off the highway and down a steep incline. She covered her face with her arms as the snow flew towards the windshield. A sudden stop inflated the airbag; the seat belt cut into her abdomen and chest. As she pushed the remnants of the deflated bag away from her face, her first thought was to turn off the motor.

Only the wind and the faint whisper of the falling snow broke the silence. The darkness overwhelmed her. Above the sound of the wind, she heard an engine roar into reverse. Maybe he hadn't intended to run her off. Perhaps she should switch on the light to show she was alive. But what, she thought frantically, what if he wanted to kill her? One person was already dead. A light flashed in her rearview mirror. He shone a flashlight towards her. Anne let her head fall back as the light hit her car. It played through the window for long minutes before it left her in darkness again. Not daring to breathe, she waited for the sound of the engine to reach her. He was gone. The darkness closed in again. She switched on the lights.

The cold crept into the car. She'd better turn on the engine. How much time had passed? She knew she drifted in and out. Did the battery have enough juice?

When she cranked the engine, the lights dimmed, and it didn't catch. She'd leave the lights on, she thought. Maybe someone would see her. It was so cold.

Adam and Brad drove along the highway to the inn road. They passed no one going the other way and found nothing by the time they reached the inn and found out Anne left as the snow began. A quick call to Catherine wasn't reassuring. Anne still hadn't returned.

They drove along the lane towards the highway in gathering darkness. There still had been no sign of Anne's vehicle when they turned from the lane to the main road. Brad used the searchlight on the shoulders.

"Stop, stop. Someone's gone over. I can see a light down the slope here," Brad shouted.

Adam slid down the slope. Behind him, Brad called fire and rescue. Ahead, Anne's head twisted, visible in the faint light from the dashboard. When he called her name, one hand gestured and fell. her hand.

He pulled at the driver's side door, but it was jammed. The passenger door opened and he crawled inside.

"Are you hurt?"

"From the seatbelt and airbag, I think. I have a headache, but I don't have any pains in my legs, and I can feel everything. I'm cold, Adam. Please get me out of here."

"Do you think, if I help you, you could crawl over the console?"

"I can try."

Anne lifted herself across to the other bucket seat.

"I won't be able to walk up. I feel too faint."

Anne's voice faded as did the color from her face. Adam scanned the hill for any sign of the rescue vehicles. The slope rose at a steep angle, rutted from the recent rains and deep with snow. The temperature was falling, and the wind was picking up. She was right. They weren't going to walk up without help.

Adam settled Anne back in the car and covered her with a blanket he found in her trunk along with candles and a shovel. He made a tent of the blanket and lit the candle. It would be enough to take the chill off. Anne drifted off to sleep. He woke her as he heard the sirens. She must have a concussion he thought.

With sirens wailing and lights flashing, the rescue vehicles drew up at the top of the hill. Two firemen and a paramedic descended the slope, the stretcher attached by lines to the truck above.

The paramedic checked Anne, collared her neck, and attached his monitoring equipment. She opened her eyes, answered his questions, and drifted away again. The team transferred her to the stretcher. Fifteen minutes later, Brad slid down to the demolished car as the ambulance left.

"Shine the light on the driver's side, Brad. Anne said someone pushed her off."

The front fender was crumpled against a tree. Black paint clung to the broken metal of the pale blue car. Brad scraped a sample into the evidence bag.

"She thinks it was a Jeep," Adam said.

"There only are about ten black Jeeps locally."

"If it is local."

"I'll put out an all points on a black SUV, likely a Jeep, with damage to the passenger side, possibly marked with blue paint," Brad said, as they reached the top and got back in the cruiser.

"Get me a list of local Jeeps, too."

Adam picked up a vehicle at the station and drove to the hospital. Anne had been admitted for observation. Her eyes were closed when he walked in, but she opened them and smiled up at him.

"Thank you. You saved my life today."

"You're welcome," he said, "but it was my deputy who saw your lights."

"I appreciate you staying with me."

"No trouble, ma'am. How are you feeling?"

Adam smiled down at her. He was a little alarmed at her color. She was pale, to begin with and now looked ashen against the white hospital sheets.

"Headache, nausea, sleepy. About what you would expect. They are coming to get me for a cat scan in a minute. Adam, what do I know that anyone would want to kill me for?"

"It must be in those files you have been working on."

"I haven't found anything yet."

"Someone thinks you have or you might. Who knows you're helping me?"

"The whole diner. One of the twins called out to me this morning, asking was I helping you. I am sure my face gave me away before I could shush him. I'm sorry."

"No, I'm sorry. You're the one in danger. I'm leaving someone outside your door until you are released."

"Thanks, Adam."

Anne squeezed his hand and went back to sleep, only to waken with a startle that shook her body as she relived the impact. Perhaps she should go home, she thought, as she drifted into sleep again.

Chapter Twelve

S unday promised a peach of a day: crisp air, bright blue skies, with the temperature rising into spring range. Adam drove out to the hospital to see Anne. A two-story, red brick structure built around an atrium replaced the Victorian mansion plus additions that served the town up until two years before. Anne's room was on the second floor.

"Come in, Adam. I've found an old friend. Brad Murdock, Adam Davidson."

"Old friend?" asked Adam as he shook Dr. Murdock's hand.

"Yes, we trained together for a year in Toronto."

"Anne and I were gossiping about old times, Lieutenant. I've got rounds, Anne. Could we have dinner before you leave town?"

"Sure, I'd be happy to. I'm being discharged," she said, turning happily to Adam.

"Good, Brad will drive you home."

"I can take a taxi."

"No, I don't want you alone. The twins promised to stay on guard all day."

"All right. I'd hate to disappoint the boys. You think it was deliberate?"

Anne clutched at her blanket as she watched Adam's face.

"It looks like it from your car. Do you remember who was at the diner yesterday morning?" he asked as he pulled a chair up to the bedside.

"No one I knew except Dougal and Peg. Maybe they would remember. One guy stared at me after Dougal spoke."

"What did he look like?"

"Short, stocky, muscular, red hair, clean shaven. That's about all."

"Good, I think I can place him."

Brad knocked at the door and came in to take Anne home.

Adam drove out along County Road 11 to the Beauchamp home. The family lived in the area for many generations. They, too, claimed ancestry direct from France, not through Quebec.

What was it with these people? What difference did it make if a man made a detour before he settled in America? Come to think of it, this family claimed some sort of French nobility too. Not too many princes settling around Vermont border towns in the 1700's.

Adam stopped in front of one of the few stone houses in that part of the state, a square, two-story building with deeply-recessed windows and a bright blue door. It was early for calling on a Sunday, but a barking dog and the pealing of the doorbell brought a sulky maid. A Vermont girl by her accent, she hadn't quite acquired the correct manner for opening the door.

"Lieutenant Davidson, Culver's Mills Police," Adam said as he displayed his identification. "Could I speak to Mrs. Beauchamp, please?"

"None of the family's finished breakfast, yet."

Apparently, this meant a mere policeman couldn't disturb them.

"You best tell Mrs. Beauchamp I'm here."

Adam's official manner and tone brought an immediate response. The young girl left him twirling his hat in the hallway. This house had been altered, opened up, painted light colors. There were several bright but obscure, at least to Adam, modern paintings on the wall. Maybe Erin could tell him what this decorating style was supposed to be.

"Mr. Davidson, could you follow me?"

The maid showed him into a corner room. Three women around a table set in a bay window. He knew Mrs. Andrea Beauchamp, a tall, thin, silver-haired woman with large brown eyes and a prominent, slightly hooked nose. The two people with her were quite a bit younger, both girls, grand-daughters maybe.

"Good morning, Detective."

They met when burglars struck the house, several years before.

"Good morning, Mrs. Beauchamp."

"Would you like coffee?"

She indicated a seat at the end of the table.

"Yes, thank you, ma'am. "

Mrs. Beauchamp introduced her granddaughters, Claire and Cecilia, home from university. Both girls had their grandmother's dark hair and large eyes.

"Mrs. Beauchamp, have you heard about Jennifer Smith's death?"

Her composed features didn't change in their expression.

"Yes, what a tragedy. She was helpful to me in researching my husband's family."

"Had she finished?"

"She had barely started. Of course, we have some family records, but the early ancestors left little."

"Any surprises?"

The coffee here was perfect too, he thought as he waited for her reply.

"Surprises?"

"Anything you hadn't expected to find. Anything embarrassing—you know—a horse thief or a Canadian or something?"

"Good heavens, no. Why do you ask?"

There was a genuine surprise in her voice.

"We discovered Jennifer had unexpected income. We wonder if she tried to blackmail some of the people she worked for."

"Certainly not us. After all, one lives in the present, not the past. If she had suggested such a thing, I would have called you immediately."

"And your children?"

Adam knew the girls' father was a proud man.

"Jennifer reported to me."

She waved away the suggestion.

"What about the cousin in Montreal who started the inquiry? Didn't she report to her?"

A slight frown flickered on the old lady's face and was gone.

"I don't know to whom you refer. I only started with Jennifer two weeks ago. If she was working on our family for someone else, I didn't know about it."

"The woman's name is Nicole Bouchard."

"She's a cousin, but I haven't spoken to her in a long time."

"Is Mr. Thomas Beauchamp here, Mrs. Beauchamp?"

"No, he's in New York for the week. I can't believe any blackmailing has gone on in my family. None of us would stand for it. Is that all?"

"Yes, ma'am." Adam knew when enough was enough. "I'll call back to see your son."

~

Adam called at the Culvers but found no one at home, not even the quiet housekeeper who wanted to talk to him. Maybe they all went to church, he thought.

At the station, Pete was in, filing a report on his Burlington interviews. He stayed overnight at his brother's because of the storm. The Culvers' alibis were good, at least the Burlington part. Careful Pete checked at the restaurant.

As for the Utronskis, they hadn't seen any of Jennifer's money. They lived a modest lifestyle in a quiet suburb. The husband taught at the local college; the wife was a nurse who worked part-time. They had a mortgage, drove cars that were several years old and sent their kids to public school. Pete felt they could eliminate them as suspects.

It was Brad's day off, but he too plodded through the files, trying to recover more of Jennifer's work.

Adam sat back in his office chair, throwing paper balls at his wastebasket, trying to sum up and get some kind of picture of the case. So far, they placed no one at the scene, save that anonymous grey car. No one admitted to being worried about Jennifer's research. No paper trail led to the money in the safety deposit box. He still needed to talk to Davis again. That lawyer was so slick he'd slide in his own footprints. Maybe Anne could find something more in those files. He needed to talk to the teller in the bank in Burlington. Did Jennifer stay with the relatives when she went down to deposit the money or in a hotel? If at a hotel, did anyone meet with her?

"Boss." Pete was calling him.

"What?"

Adam brought his feet down off the desk.

"I'm going home unless you need me."

"No, go home."

As far as Adam could tell, it was going to take days of work to try and make a connection between Jennifer and whomever she was bleeding for money, one of whom who may or may not have murdered her. Pete might as well start again tomorrow.

Adam went out to Catherine's to talk to Anne. Maybe the ancestor-trolling did hold the answer to the crime. He found Anne and Catherine in the garden, shaking heavy snow from evergreens and checking buds on the crab apples. He happily accepted an invitation to stay for lunch. He hoped it was Catherine's well-known Sunday brunch.

As he tucked into eggs Benedict, Georgia ham and homemade scones, he questioned Anne again about genealogy research.

"If you were researching the Beauchamps, how would you start if you wanted to find blackmail material?"

Anne stopped eating her eggs to give the question her attention.

"That's not something I had given much thought to before I came here. But I've thought that if you started with the family's own history or legend, you check backwards in the way we do in genealogy. For example, the Beauchamps have lived here for two hundred years, about seven generations. The first two or three should be obvious and clear, but I would look for birth records, marriage certificates, and death records starting at the grandparents. Do you know anything about them?"

Anne picked up her fork again.

"Here's the hard copy of Jennifer's research. It starts with the cousin in Montreal. She didn't have a separate file for Mrs. Beauchamp."

"Yes, you see this cousin claims to be the daughter of Andrea Beauchamp's husband John's brother Peter. So her grandparents on her father's side would be the local ones here. They were called Andre and Marie. Marie was a Canadian from Montreal. Her surname was Cloutier. Now that is an old Quebec "pur laine" name. It looks like she was born there in 1901. If so she might be listed in the census of 1901.

"How do you know there was a census in 1901?"

Adam was curious that she would be so sure of the year.

"A census in Canada is taken every ten years on the ones—1851,61,71,91,01,11. I would check in the 1901 and see if I could find any record. If I couldn't find her in the census, I would send for a birth record. The death record here would give her birth date."

Anne looked longingly at her cooling eggs.

"Why so much checking."

"It is important to be sure people were identified, especially if you put the information in the public domain, on the net. Many people use it, including the Mormons for religious reasons, and it's got to be correct."

"How much further back can you go?"

"The Beauchamp's family goes back four generations beyond that, so I would check as much as I could. For example, I found an old diary at the library that belonged to a woman named Beauchamp. I believe she was connected to the local family, but I would do more checking. I would also make sure all the children were accounted for with birth or baptismal certificates. If I wanted to blackmail, I would look for other things as well. Family gossip, local gossip, items in newspapers. She may have started with someone local who could tell her old stories. Do you know anyone like that?"

"A few, starting with Peg Watson and Ada Warren."

Adam swallowed the last bit of coffee, said his thanks and left. Anne looked at her hostess who was bringing her eggs to replace the ones that had gone cold.

"I hope Ada's had her lunch," Anne said.

Adam put off talking to Ada and Maud. Time to go home, feed the cat, and take care of chores. Soon, he thought, he would be at the stage of either do laundry or buy new underwear.

Chapter Thirteen

H eavy cold rain pounded down in the early hours of Monday and by dawn, washed away all but the dirty black remnants of the snow banks. The sun promised to eliminate those. Maybe they'd get some spring, after all, Adam thought as he drove into the square. The diner would be a good place to start this morning.

"Coffee, eggs, bacon and toast please, Peg."

Mondays were busy with most of the business people in town dropping in for coffee or breakfast on the way to work. Adam lingered over his second cup of coffee until business slowed down. Peg came over to pour him a refill.

"You want something, Adam?"

"Why do you ask?"

"You never stay this long."

"You're right. I wondered if you knew the stories about the Beauchamps and the Culvers?"

"You mean the old gossip."

"Yeah, I think so. Whatever happened, it was before 1900."

"No, I don't think so. I heard it was the one who was Andre Beauchamp's grandfather, the one whose picture is in the library."

"I don't know about the picture."

"Behind the main desk."

"What gossip did you hear?"

Peg paused her cleaning to consider his question.

"You have to remember, I wasn't born here. My husband and I came here after he got out of the army. People don't tell me as much as they would if my family had lived here for a long time."

Peg raised her eyebrows and Adam nodded.

"I do hear things said. Anyway, it's not gossip when the information is that old. More like local history. I hear there were scandals, and maybe a suicide. That's when the Beauchamps stopped mixing in town. They haven't sent their kids to local schools or married here since then. I don't know why they stayed."

"That's all? You don't know what the scandal was?"

"No idea."

"Thanks, Peg. See you tomorrow."

Disappointed, Adam left. On his way to the office, he dropped by the library. He hadn't seen a picture of Andre Beauchamp behind the desk because it wasn't there. Watercolor sketches of the town filled the space. He asked Nancy Webb about the portrait. She said Jennifer had suggested the change a few months ago. Nancy thought the picture had gone into storage. No, she wasn't sure. Yes, she would check when she wasn't busy, working without her computer. Didn't like her then, didn't like her now, Adam thought.

Adam and Pete met at the office. Pete attended court for the wrap-up testimony of a recent case. Brad worked at the computer and expected Anne in to help him. Adam suggested they concentrate today on Andre and Marie Beauchamp, telling Brad what he learned so far. Adam was going to Burlington to see the bankers and to interview Stan Davis again on the way.

Ted Atkins followed Adam out the door of Lil's. He'd been too far away to hear much of the conversation between Peg and Adam, but enough to know Adam asked questions about the town's two wealthiest families, one of which, the Culvers, owned the paper he worked for.

The reporter loped across the square in time to see Adam enter the courthouse. He waited on the steps, smoking one of his many cigarettes of the day, for Adam to come out. He butted out in a convenient plant stand as Adam came down the steps.

"Adam, what's this about the Beauchamps and the Culvers? How do they figure in your investigation?"

Careful, Adam told himself. He's fishing.

"What about them?"

"I heard you were asking questions about them. Are they involved in the murder? The people want to know."

"Tell the people our investigations are proceeding. Don't make me regret talking to you."

"Come on."

"I have work to do."

Adam slammed his car door and started his engine.

Adam always enjoyed the drive to Greenbank. His humor slowly recovered as he drove along the road that followed the curve of the river, sometimes close enough to see it, sometimes separated by a farm or an estate. Trees overhung the narrow country road. Where the trees expanded into small woods, he caught the occasional flash of white from an early flowering tree, a wild plum or maybe serviceberry. White or brown slatted fences, the type that meant horses, not cattle, surrounded the homes set in fifty to one hundred acre farms. In summer, every house looked as though it sat in a golf green.

Greenbank was a corridor town: a few houses, a mall, some service offices and a gas station. It existed because the countryside around it contained those large estates whose wealthy owners at times needed someone local to handle emergencies like a speeding ticket or a head cold.

Davis and O'Connor were in reality just Davis, in a corner office in the strip mall. The office was still closed Monday until ten o'clock. At 9:59am a young woman clattered up the sidewalk and Adam followed her into the office.

"Help you?" she said as she hung up her coat revealing a too tight, too short skirt over legs and hips that should have remained a mystery.

Adam showed her his badge, watched her vacant blue eyes open wide. Surely a lawyer's secretary had police visits before.

"I don't think Mr. Davis is in yet," she said, turning nervously toward the back of the office.

"Could you see?"

"Sure."

Two doors other than the one to the outside opened off the reception area. She pushed open the left-hand door, stepped in, and emerged, screaming. Adam pushed past her.

Davis, his body anyway, sat in his chair, his forehead marked by a bullet hole almost dead center. Adam called the emergency number. He took the secretary out of the room and got her calmed enough to talk.

"When did you last see Davis alive Miss—"

"Ashley Baines is my name. I saw him on Friday afternoon when I was leaving for the day." She paused to blow her nose. "He'd just come back from Burlington."

"Did he seem okay? Did you notice anything different or unusual?"

"Not different, except he sort of rushed me out."

"What do you mean?"

"I was being kind of slow, I guess. I put on a little makeup and brushed my hair before I put on my coat. He was irritable with me, you know, asking me if I was going to take all day. I wondered if someone was coming to the office that he didn't want me to know about."

"Did that happen often?"

"You mean that he rushed me out?"

"No, that he didn't want you to know who he was meeting?"

"I think so, but I'm not really sure. When was he killed?"

"Not today," Adam said.

The young woman was truthful, he thought. She was pale and jittery, but only because of the body, not because of guilt.

A cruiser turned into a parking spot in front of the office and an older man, slightly portly, blue-jeaned, wearing a bomber style jacket with *Sheriff's Office* on the back, walked in. Grey hair, grizzled face, a small chin disappearing into a larger second one: Bill Perkins, Sheriff of Langton County for the last 35 years.

"Morning Adam."

"Morning, Bill."

"What do you have for me?"

He walked past Adam when he motioned the sheriff into the next room.

"By God, Stan Davis. Someone got the bugger at last."

"What do you mean by at last, Sheriff?"

"He's had a shady reputation for years. I've suspected him of being across the line with his clients more than a few times but could never pin anything on him."

His forensics crew arrived.

"Let's talk outside while the boys work and let's send the little girl home until we need her."

Adam hustled a now-reluctant Ashley out of the door as the sheriff pulled chairs up to the desk in the outer office. Adam outlined his case to

Perkins, knowing the older man's reputation for solving some of the hard ones.

"Have you suspected him of blackmail?"

"Can't say that I have. But then folks being blackmailed usually play it pretty close. I don't know those two families you spoke of real well, although I do recall some sort of old scandal about the Beauchamps. There was some bad blood about land, I think, maybe 75 or 100 years ago now. I never learned any details."

"Can I have my computer geek have a look at the set-up here? Maybe he kept some records I could use."

"Sure. We'll want to look through for any clients who might be holding a grudge against the guy. I'll let you know the forensics on the bullet. Any guns turn up in your investigation yet?"

"Not one. I'll keep you up to date from our end."

They shook hands at the door, and Adam left to continue the drive to Burlington. Follow the money.

The manager of the Burlington Savings and Loan arranged for him to meet the tellers. They spelled each other at the wickets of the old-fashioned bank as he interviewed them in their lunchroom. They all remembered taking the deposits from Jennifer at different times. None of them remembered her saying what business she was in, but they assumed a store or a service that dealt in cash. One of the girls had the impression Jennifer was an antique dealer, another a jewelry salesperson. None knew her personally. They gave her address as the Chesterton Hotel.

The Chesterton Hotel was an unfashionable place on the edge of downtown, popular with travelling salesmen, and executives of minor companies in town for short periods. The desk clerk told him Jennifer kept a permanent room. Sure he could have the key, seeing she was dead.

The room Jennifer used for her double life looked out over a park. She had brought pictures of her family and some framed country scenes.

The bed was just a bed, but she had covered it with a colorful quilt. A crucifix hung over it. The rest of the furniture was standard hotel modern but included a microwave, apartment-sized fridge, and coffee maker. On the shelf of the only closet, he found a small file box with several computer disks—didn't anyone use paper anymore—and a daybook. The last entry was the Saturday before she died. Dinner with S.D. at Malcolm's.

Adam took the disks and the daybook. He would send someone to do a careful search, but he thought there would be little else.

Downstairs the desk clerk, more interested in a ball game on TV than the police presence, grudgingly directed him to Malcolm's, a restaurant with widely spaced tables, low lights and bored waiters. The manager and the server on duty recalled Stan and Jennifer. They were frequent customers. No, not lovers, or at least the waitress didn't think so. They seemed to do business—passing papers back and forth, sometimes envelopes. No, no money that she'd seen, and, no, they never had any other dinner guests.

Adam had opened the door to the street when the server called him back. She remembered one occasion when another person came to their table. They didn't talk while she served, but they were all angry. The extra man left without eating.

She described him as medium—height, weight, build, hair, nose—all medium, but she thought she would be able to identify him if needed. Oh, a moustache and bad skin. Great, he thought, a medium guy with a medium moustache, how easy would he be to find.

Adam remembered the Utronskis as he passed their subdivision. He had time to interview them again if they were home.

The subdivision was called Fantasy Forest. Who came up with these names?

The Utronskis lived on Enchanted Oak Lane in a smaller back split. A basketball hoop over the garage and a bike abandoned on the lawn completed the picture. A woman who said she was Mrs. Utronski answered the door.

Jennifer had been a tall, slim woman with angular features but Darlene Utronski was the reverse, fairly short, heavy with a round face that looked like it was used to being cheerful. She invited Adam into the small formal living room.

"Is there any news, Lieutenant? Do you know who killed Jennifer?"

He could hear echoes of Jennifer's voice in her sister's.

"No, ma'am. I have something to tell you that is not too good."

He paused, but she stared anxiously at him, saying nothing.

"Jennifer might have been blackmailing some people in a scheme with a man called Davis."

He watched the color drain from her face, heard the whispered "no".
She hadn't been involved, Adam thought.

"Are you sure? She was a religious woman, Lieutenant. How could she?"

"Tell me about your sister. Did she have any special need for money?"

Darlene shook her head slowly.

"All she ever did with any extra money was give it to the church. I hoped she would help us save for the children's education, but she never said anything about doing that."

"Was she always so devoted to the church?"

"Oh, no. She fell away for a long time. You see, as a young woman, she had done something awful. At least, she felt it was awful. She had an abortion. Since she came back to the Church, she has been trying to atone for it. Father O'Brien told her that she didn't need to give money, that she needed faith and to do good works, but she believed that if she gave enough money to the church itself, she would be forgiven."

"Did you find her different lately?"

Darlene dropped her head and looked at her hands for long seconds before she spoke.

"She seemed to be thinking less clearly or logically or something. She was irritable and tense with the children. She was furious with the library board in Culver's Mills because they gave the librarian's job to someone else. Overwhelmed with anger."

Darlene cried quietly, tears rolling unheeded down her cheeks.

"I think that's enough, Mrs. Utronski. Thank you for your help. I'll let you know when we have made some progress."

Adam stood up to leave, but the grieving woman didn't notice or care.

Another life shattered, he thought as he drove back to Culver's Mills. He saw Anne's rental car in the guest parking and found her with Brad, still at the computer. They found some further information on Andrew Beauchamp, but not much on his wife. Anne said she needed to go across the border to a genealogical library to look at census data in order to go further. She wondered if Adam wanted her to search the local newspaper archive for any information about the Beauchamps of that generation.

"Yes, I do. Let's leave the cross-border stuff for a little while unless you can call somebody."

"What about the Beauchamp cousin who started all this? Perhaps she knows something."

"That's a good idea. Brad, you call her with Anne at your elbow. See if she can fax you what she has."

Adam took a chair from another desk and sat down near the computers. He had to tell her.

"There has been another murder," he said. "Brad, I don't want you to leave Anne during the day, and I want you to borrow from county to guard her house at night."

"Who was killed?" Anne asked in a small tight voice.

Adam remembered that she had just recovered from her concussion. He brought her some coffee before he answered.

"A guy called Stan Davis, a lawyer. He was associated with her in some way, maybe business partners. He was shot sometime since Friday night before I could talk to him again."

"Adam, what is going on? Jennifer was an assistant librarian in a small Vermont town. Was the person with the bank accounts really her? Did you show her picture at the bank?"

Adam replied patiently. He knew Anne was frightened and confused.

"I showed the picture. Remember we found the records and the money in her own safety deposit box, and the bank here knew her well."

Anne flushed and started to apologize, but Brad covered her embarrassment by saying, "Okay, we'll call the Montreal connection of the Beauchamps. Do you think any of these people would pay up to blackmail?"

"I'm not sure yet. Are you two done for the day?"

They were finished. Anne gathered up the material she was taking back with her to work on, and they left the office. They were standing at the top of the courthouse steps when a low-slung grey sports car pulled out of a parking spot down the street and accelerated towards the courthouse. Adam turned towards the sound of the engine and saw the flash of the sun off the handgun before he heard the report. He threw Anne on the steps. A bullet pinged off the step behind them and ricocheted off the courthouse door. Adam was on his feet, running to the cruiser, yelling at Brad to get Anne inside. The grey car was out of sight, down a street that angled away from the square, and the courthouse. Adam couldn't see it as he raced the length of the road to where it became the highway. No luck and no license number.

Goddammit, he thought as he climbed the steps. Who's trying to kill her? He traced the bullet's mark on the stone of the courthouse and the chip out of the heavy oak door. He found it in a flower bed just off the steps. It was crushed. Maybe forensics could get something.

He slammed the door behind him as he strode into the office, startling

Brad and Anne, who were hunched over coffee cups. A blanket covered Anne's still shaking shoulders. Adam shook his head at Brad.

"You?"

"Grey Camaro. I think. No license on it. I'll run the locals in a minute."

"Adam, I want to go home."

"I'll take you to Catherine's."

"No, I want to go home to Canada. If I leave, they'll decide we've given up. And there aren't so many guns."

"No, whoever it is will likely follow you. Everyone in town knows who you are. Whatever this is about, the stakes must be very high."

"I can go to friends in Montreal. No one will find me there."

"How long can you hide? Anne, now that we know you definitely are a target, we can protect you. I can't protect you in Montreal or Bridgenorth. I'm selfish too. I need your help to sort this out. I'll borrow a female state trooper to stay with you and Brad will be with you all day. Please stay."

A sudden silence filled the room. Adam watched Anne's nervous hands twisting as she played with her rings.

"I can't tell you now. I'll let you know in the morning."

Anne's words squeezed past the tightness in her throat.

"All right. Whatever you decide, we'll protect you as long as you are here." Adam turned to Brad. "Here's a disk from Jennifer's room in Burlington. Lock it in evidence and work on it in the morning."

"I can stay late if you want."

"No, take Anne back to Catherine's and stay until the trooper arrives. Get the cruiser and bring it around to the back door.

Adam watched them go and then left for home. He had to call Erin and confirm for Tuesday night. It would be great to be with her, but he wasn't sure he would be welcome at the little theater wrap-up party. He and his men had interrogated several of the cast members and the host of the party.

Chapter Fourteen

Adam swung by Catherine's on his way into the office the next morning. Maggie bounded from the porch to meet him, her wiggling back end and wagging tail betraying the black lab in her ancestry. Adam scratched her ears as he waited at the screen door.

"Morning, Catherine. Could I speak to Anne a moment?" he asked as she held the door open for him.

"Sure, come on in. Brad is already here."

Catherine's house always smelled good, like home did when his mother was alive. This morning the aroma was coffee and sausage with the added sharp scent of oranges and cinnamon from freshly baked muffins. Brad and Anne sat at one end of the long pine harvest table, drinking coffee from oversized bright blue mugs. The remains of their breakfast were still on the table. Adam sat down in one of the mismatched press-backed chairs.

"Morning," Adam said as Catherine put down coffee and a plate of sausage and eggs in front of him.

"Thanks. What are your plans for the day?" he asked Anne.

"I'm going to the office with Brad, wearing one of your protective vests. He says to wear it or stay in. So I caved to the pressure."

Anne's light words didn't reflect the dark circles and taut lines around her eyes. Nightmares of bullets and menacing anonymous vehicles had bothered her sleep. When Anne worried, she woke at 4:00am. Always. She called them her ugly hours, four to six. Whatever the worst might be, she could imagine it. Eventually, she would sleep a little. Morning usually brought a decision.

And so it had been this morning. Though she was afraid to stay, she was more reluctant to go. If she left, she knew she would be spending many more early mornings worrying, checking her doors, always fearing who might be waiting for her. She didn't want to be anybody's loose end.

Beyond all that, she was a problem solver. If she had the key to the mystery, she'd stay.

Adam was talking to her. "He's right."

"I know, I know."

"When you reach the office, pull into the judges' parking. Call Pete to meet you and cover you while you go in."

Fear filled her throat with nausea. She should go home.

"Perhaps we'll find the answer in the files today."

"Sure."

Adam stood up and thanked Catherine as he left.

At the office, Adam picked up his file on the Beauchamps to have a quick read before he drove on out to their estate. There hadn't been anything added that would help him in the interview.

The day was another sunny one, spring temperatures and the earthy smell that meant the end of winter to him. The melting snow left only a few patches on the soaked and flattened lawn at the entrance to the Beauchamps. He wanted to talk to Thomas Beauchamp today. The matriarch certainly wasn't going to give him the time of day, and he didn't have anything to pry her open with.

The young maid hadn't improved her attitude any. Maybe she wasn't a morning person, he thought.

"Mr. Beauchamp can't be disturbed."

"I think you better, missy. I don't want to come back with a warrant."

Strange how that threat almost always got results.

"Mr. Davidson."

Thomas Beauchamp, heir to the Beauchamp fortune, businessman, and world-class skier as a young man was a lithe and tanned fifty, not tall, with his mother's black eyes and prominent nose. He took Adam into the library where he had spoken to the senior Mrs. Beauchamp on his last visit. Adam got right to it when they sat down.

"Mr. Beauchamp, I would like to ask you some questions about Jennifer Smith and a woman called Nicole Bouchard."

"Nicole's one of my more distant cousins in Montreal. What can you possibly want to know about her?"

His surprise seemed genuine enough.

"She had been using Jennifer to research your family."

"You mean Jennifer had been charging my mother and Nicole for the same work?"

"That's the least of what she had been doing. I have to ask you, sir, if Jennifer blackmailed you or any member of your family."

Adam knew the answer might well be a lie, but that was useful sometimes.

"Certainly not. Not only that, there is nothing anyone could blackmail us about. My mother told you, I think."

"What about this story of Andrew Beauchamp's second family."

"What about it? The story's been around for years. True or not, it doesn't affect us. We are sophisticated people, Lieutenant. Most families as old as ours have a bastard or two. It doesn't matter if the wills are written correctly and ours always are."

"What do you know about Nicole?"

"Not much. She's some kind of second or third cousin. I only met her once; at a funeral, I think."

"We'll be contacting her."

"By all means. As I said, it doesn't concern us. If that's all?"

"Not quite. What vehicles do you own? And what color are they?"

"A black Mercedes sedan, a red Porsche and one of those little Neons for the staff to use for errands. It's red also. I have an old silver Honda Prelude as well."

Adam stood up, shook hands, and left with as little information as he came with and no grounds at all for a warrant to search. He'd try to get some financial information from gossip central at the diner at lunch.

At the station, Brad checked the files on Jennifer's disk. When Adam came in, he called him over.

"I think I got something, boss, but she's used code names with amounts beside them."

"How many names?"

"Ten, but some of them are inactive now. Do blackmailers quit?"

"When the well is dry. What kind of code did Jennifer use?"

"Odd. First, there is a name, then a year and a month, followed by a sum. The names are strange, not people or cities or anything like that."

"What does Anne think?"

"I haven't shown her yet."

Anne was deep into what looked to be land records on microfilm. Brad had borrowed the set-up from the library over Nancy Webb's protests, subdued by asking her if she wanted Anne to die in her library too. Anne took a break from the tedious perusal of records to look at Brad's list.

"Those are immigrant ships' names," she said.

"Immigrant ships?" Brad said.

"Yes, the immigrants to this country came mostly on ships until recently. Now they come on planes or across the borders with Mexico or Canada. There are ships' passenger lists for many of them. For example, you take the first one, the Samaria. She was a ship that ran between Europe and Canada. I have two friends who came on her as children, one Dutch, one Slovak. The year and month likely refer to arrivals. Maybe blackmail subject was on the ship?"

Anne read the rest of the list and shook her head.

"No, that can't be right. Some of these ships were the coffin ships."

"Coffin ships?" Adam said.

"Yes, they brought starving Irish immigrants from about 1845 on. Here's the Galway in 1852. I wonder if Jennifer looked until she found a name on a list that was the same as her victim and used a cross-reference to encode it. Brad, pull up the database she had of ships' passenger lists. Look for the Samaria."

Brad spent a few minutes finding the list and the month. Most of the passengers had been Dutch, but he did see one name he thought had been on Jennifer's client list. After cross-checking, he gave Adam the name David Hanson, address in New York City. Across from the entry they thought referred to him was a small sum—$500. With luck, he would admit to being blackmailed.

"Try and find someone a little closer to home, Brad. I don't want to go to New York this weekend."

"Okay, but it'll take us some time."

"I'm going to go back to old records and newspapers," Anne told him. "You said there was supposed to be some land problem in the early 1900's."

"So I heard, but what the details were, I have no idea."

"I'm going to work backwards from what the Culvers and the Beauchamps own now to see if there was any conflict or dispute.

"Fine."

The phone rang in Adam's office. Bill Perkins' lab had compared the bullet that killed Davis with the one that had slammed into the wall behind Anne. No direct comparison was possible because the bullet was so flattened, but they were the same caliber.

A witness saw a guy with a big moustache drive away from the strip mall where Davis had died late Friday. Other description—medium. The vehicle was described as a black SUV, like a Jeep. Plate number—of course not.

The medical examiner placed the time of death as likely on Friday but could get no closer because of the delay in finding the body.

Adam told Bill about his no-help interview with Beauchamps and about cracking the computer code and promised to keep in touch.

It was lunchtime, and Adam promised to send food over for his hard-working researchers. Spring was definitely coming, he thought as he walked across the square to Lil's. Clumps of bright yellow daffodils dotted the formal garden beds of the green. A robin perched on the heroic figure of a founding father in the center of the square.

Adam bounded up the steps into Lil's and settled himself at the counter of the diner. He loved the time-warp feel of the place, the chrome and the red leatherette. Peg had kept the big neon sign outside and one spelling Coca-cola over the mirror. She bought the place lock, stock and beautiful old milk-shake machine. She also made great chicken salad sandwiches with French fries. Adam had two.

"Peg, what do you hear about the Beauchamps and money?" Adam said as he finished his meal.

"They have a lot," Peg said, raising an eyebrow in a question.

"Do you hear anything else, any money worries, any bad debts? Are they paying their bills on time and the staff wages?"

"People like that always pay bills a month late, and they're no different. The staff hasn't complained in here about money. Saucy little Tracey complains about how she is mistreated, but I haven't heard her say anything serious."

"Tracey?"

"You know, the maid. She probably opened the front door for you, one job she hates."

"That shows. I wondered what was biting her."

"The way I hear it she thinks she is a Beauchamp, that her great-grandmother and Andrew Beauchamp were lovers and the family got cut out of the inheritance

"What's she doing working for them? Do they know that?"

"Probably not. None of them talk to people around here."

"What's her last name?"

"Dirkens. Her mother was a Sinclair."

"Do you know the great-grandmother's name?"

"No... yes, I do. Agatha Spotiswood. When I first came to town, I volunteered at the county home. I remember Tracey and her grandmother coming in every Sunday to see her.

"What about the family, brothers, uncles. Is any one of them a hothead or the type to carry a grudge a long time?"

"No, there's only Tracey. Her dad left before she was born, her mother died in a car accident a couple of years later and the grandmother Sinclair brought her up. Mrs. Sinclair died two years ago. Tracey's about twenty now. She has attitude, but she has never been a violent kid."

"What about cousins, other descendants of this Spotiswood."

"Don't know. There weren't many in the family, or so I have always been led to believe. It's sad she's so alone."

"Thanks, Peg, see you later."

Adam picked up the order to go and crossed to the courthouse. Anne listened to the story of the maid and her lineage while she ate her take-out lunch. She told Adam she would look for Spotiswood relatives. Adam looked up Tracey Dirkens' home address. She lived at the Beauchamp estate. He wondered how resentful Tracey was, working as a servant in what she believed to be her great-grandmother's house. If she believed it. He'd send Pete out to ask her.

Brad had called Nicole Bouchard in Montreal. She was young sounding, about thirty, he thought, and she spoke heavily-accented English. Anne could speak passable French and volunteered to interpret for Brad.

Nicole claimed to be searching the Vermont Beauchamps for completeness, and to see if Jennifer could find anything for her before 1850. She wasn't interested in offshoots of the family tree that weren't legitimate. One fact she thought she had was a marriage between a Beauchamp daughter and a Culver son in 1916. Leticia and Douglas were their names. Anne hadn't come across them as yet. Nicole denied being blackmailed.

"Certainement, non."

The crash of the phone into the cradle almost drowned out her hissed "merde".

"Whew, she is one hot-tempered lady. Maybe I should check if she's been across the border."

Brad was onto immigration as he spoke. Anne returned to checking land records.

Paper piled itself haphazardly on Adam's desk, and he spent the afternoon clearing it and writing a report for his boss on the progress of the investigation.

He answered calls from the local radio and television stations and Ted Atkins again. Ted's paper was due to go to press the next day, and he wanted Adam to confirm the blackmailing rumors. Adam called to say he would see him at the end of the day at Barclay's, a small pub at the corner of the square and Hunter.

He put the report on Captain Naismith's desk and walked out to where Anne was sitting, bleary-eyed from staring at microfiche all day.

"Anything?"

"No, I have checked these land deals back to the mid-twenties. Both these families managed to hold on to their property during the depression, God knows how. Did they do any smuggling?"

"Smuggling?"

"Yes, you know, liquor during prohibition for the Canadian liquor companies. A few American families, especially on the border, made or held onto their money that way."

"Not that I know," Adam said.

Brad was still clicking away from one passenger list to another.

"I've got three files, but the money is small, and the people aren't local: Alaska, Miami and one in Goose Bay, in Labrador. Do you want me to follow these up?"

"I doubt our killer paid a visit from Labrador. Give them up."

"Good, I'm out of here for today."

"Take Anne home, will you?"

"Sure."

This time they made a careful, rear door exit.

Atkins was waiting for him when Adam got to the pub. A shot and a beer sat untouched in front of him. The first or the fifth, Adam wondered, as he ordered plain soda for himself.

The first, he decided, as he talked to Atkins. Ted didn't show any signs of too much alcohol or even those of a carefully-controlled chronic drinker.

"Adam, I have a problem."

"Yeah?"

"You're investigating my boss. This blackmail stuff is out in the community, and we have to print. How much is there that involves the Culvers?"

"I'm not going to give you information for you to feed to the Culvers, Ted."

"Hell, no, but I want to keep my job. I don't want to print anything about them if I can get away without putting them in it."

"Leave out the names. Anyone else you name is going to be unhappy too, and it sure won't help me. We don't have it all anyway."

"Can I talk to Dr. McPhail?"

"About how Jennifer did it, not who she did it too, and only if she wants to. I don't think she's eager to talk to the press. Brad can give you some of it."

"Okay. That'll do. But I have to leave the Culvers out. You won't give it to Burlington or to the TV stations?"

"I won't, no."

So that was it. Didn't want to print it himself, and didn't want to be scooped either.

"I have to go, Ted."

"Thanks."

Adam left him staring glumly at his untouched drinks.

At home, Adam changed into sweats for his first run in a week. His route took him out of town, across one bridge and back in. He enjoyed the view of the river and the weir at the Mill. There was talk of renovating the mill into a restaurant, art gallery, and theatre complex. He hoped it went ahead, even if an increase in tourism brought more policing problems.

Sunset was fading when he got home. Sam was meowing pitifully. A cat can sound abandoned entirely when it's missed its meal by an hour. He fed her and realized he'd better hurry if he was going to pick Erin up at seven.

Chapter Fifteen

E rin wanted to try a new restaurant called Evan's, that had opened in an old house across the square from her store. Some of her antiques had furnished the foyer and small bar. On the way, she told Adam about the place.

"They renovated the entire house, replacing all the electric and plumbing, but saving every scrap of original molding, staircase, everything. They live upstairs."

"Do you know them well?"

"Only as customers. He's the chef. She's a graphic designer and still does a lot of work from home."

The foyer was tiny with a glowing oriental rug in the center of the hardwood floor. A pine drop-leaf table stood under a primitive, portrait painting. On the table, a polished pine bowl held a collection of ceramic balls.

"What are these, Erin?"

Before she could answer, the hostess appeared and took them into the small lounge. Erin pointed out wingback chairs and an étagère that came from her shop.

They settled in the chairs in front of a stone fireplace. Adam asked for a Bloody Caesar, a Canadian drink made with spices, clam juice, tomato juice and vodka he enjoyed on a Montreal trip. Erin had a Campari and soda.

"Those balls in the wooden bowl?"

"Those are called carpet balls. The Victorians used them for an indoor game. Mary and Tom took all I had in the shop. But you must have seen at least one before?"

"No, I don't think so."

"Jennifer Smith used a blue and white diamond patterned one for a paper-weight on her desk at the library. Could it have been taken as evidence?"

"No, I looked at everything at the station. How heavy are they?"

"Heavy."

Adam slipped back into the foyer and hefted one of the balls. The medical examiner had described the murder weapon as a smooth, round object. One of these would be perfect. Good weight too. He took an experimental strike to the astonishment of some arriving guests. He returned the ball to the collection and joined Erin who was now in the dining room.

The renovator combined the old front parlor and the sitting room of the house into a long narrow dining room. Sometime in the Victorian era, an ornate fireplace had been added at one end. Massive dark oak, ornately carved, framed a mirror above a mantle of the same wood. Bright green tiles surrounded the firebox. A broad, flat stone, worn with age, formed the hearth. A fire glowed behind tall brass firedogs.

Erin's table was at one side, set into an alcove. She sat with her back to the room. Her brown hair glowed with red highlights from the candles and firelight. Adam stood still for a moment, before joining her, for the pleasure of looking at her.

"So?"

"Later," he said as the server arrived.

Adam didn't recognize the server. New to town with the restaurant, he guessed. As she tacked across the room, she reminded Adam of the figurehead on a ship, head and chest thrust forward, her tight dark jacket emphasizing her more than ample curves. She told them her name was Matilde.

"They typed the specials and put them in the menu. I don't like taking a memory test every time I go out to dinner."

"I find that irritating, too. Everyone at the table forgets something, and the waiter goes around the table again. I know it's supposed to be more elegant."

"Do you see anything you like?"

"Yes, blackened catfish."

"Steak for me."

Their dinner was a success. The conversation ranged from the presidential primaries to their favorite music. They both enjoyed jazz and disliked modern atonal. As dessert arrived, Erin asked Adam about his family. She remembered when his parents had died in a plane crash, about two years before.

"Do you have brothers and sisters?"

"Not a one. Nor cousins, never a wife. I do have an aunt in New York. How about you?"

"Oh, I have everybody. My parents live in Burlington. My brother and his wife and kids live here. We grew up in Burlington, but I wanted to try a smaller town for my business."

"Lucky you. I miss having a family."

After a pause, she asked, "What about the carpet ball?"

"Could be. One of them is blue and white patterned. Would you look at it and tell me if it is similar to the one Jennifer had?"

"Sure. Would you like to have coffee at the shop?"

"Very much."

On their way out, Erin examined the collection of balls. She thought Jennifer's had been similar to the blue and white one, but a darker blue.

They walked in comfortable silence across the dark square. When Erin switched on the shop lights, Adam saw she had arranged chairs, lamps and a low table in front of the fireplace.

"This is nice, Erin. What are the chairs called?"

"Oh, these are more modern than usual—1930's art deco club chairs. The chrome and glass table is deco also, following a design by Eileen Grey. Would you prefer a drink?"

"Coffee, thanks."

The rest of the evening passed in quiet conversation. When Adam left, he kissed Erin softly.

"I'll call you," he said.

"I'd like that."

Chapter Sixteen

Anne worked on the computer when Adam arrived at the office in the morning. She'd changed her working clothes from sedate suits in darker colors to jeans and pullovers that matched Brad's habitually casual wear.

"Adam, I found a local name. Jake Morrison. Brad says he's a developer and he handed over quite a bit of cash."

"Good, now can you look through the land records, the most recent ones first, to see if you can find out what he owns and if it has any relationship to anyone else's on our list."

"I'm going to see if I can find out anything about the lost Culver-Beauchamp connection. Brad can do the land stuff."

"I need the help on this land deal. The Culver-Beauchamp connection can wait."

"Brad can do it. I'm not interested in routine police work. I'm only interested in genealogy."

"You could do it faster, and I need the answers."

"Don't push, Adam. I'm helping you, remember, not working for you."

"If you want to help, then help. Following the money trail will give us more answers than finding out who married who."

"If you don't want my help with the genealogy, perhaps I should go home and forget it. Brad is more competent than I am to look at land records. Or hire a real estate agent instead."

They stared at each other, appalled at the turn the conversation had taken.

Adam spoke first, relieving the tense silence. "I have no claim on your time. If you want to stop helping the investigation, say so."

"No, I want to continue, but let me follow my own leads. I don't take instruction well. Also, I'm only interested in the part of this that relates to genealogy. "

"But this Jake Morrison is a hot one."

"True, for a policeman, not a genealogist."

"Fair enough."

Brad sat behind his own computer, hiding a grin. It wasn't often he heard the boss put in his place.

"Do you want me to interview Morrison, or chase down his land deals, Lieutenant?"

"The land deals for now. Any luck on that list of grey or silver sports cars?"

"About fifty in the county fit the description. No one we've talked about is on the list."

"Did you check for priors on the owners?"

"Yes. One of them belongs to a guy who did time for assault. He's out now. I found an address from before he went away."

"Where's Pete? He can check it out."

"Pete went to meet with Bill Perkin's boys to take back the computer disks."

"Did Pete talk to Tracey Dirkens yet?"

"He put a report on your desk."

Adam poured himself a coffee and sat down to read Pete's report.

Pete had quite a time with Tracey. She told Pete her grandmother knew they were not related to that family and she, Tracey, wouldn't want to be a relative of such a boring, stuck-up bunch. They paid well, and she was saving up to leave Culver's Mills forever. She claimed she knew nothing at all about her great-grandmother. Her grandmother was ashamed that everyone thought she was Andrew Beauchamp's child and insisted it wasn't true. She knew her father was Derek Spotiswood, a soldier who died in the Great War.

Adam gave the information to Anne, who would check the databases Jennifer had collected for birth certificates. She searched as well for the elusive Douglas and Leticia Culver and any offspring. Nothing so far. She intended to look for marriages in the years after the war in a series of books which cross-referenced births, marriages and deaths in announcements in the local newspaper for 1890 to 1930. If the wedding or engagement had been announced she thought she would find it. She would look for Spotis-wood also.

At noon, Adam left for Burlington after reporting to Captain Naismith. Wednesday was the day for his law classes, one in the afternoon, the other from seven to nine at night. He found just enough time in the last week to do the reading, but he wasn't sure if he could continue to carry both, the final two courses in the first year of his part-time law degree. He had to meet with his faculty advisor early in the afternoon.

∿

Anne spent the afternoon with the records from the newspapers. She found one of a Spotswood marriage in 1916, and the notice of the man's death in France a year and a half later. Mrs. Spotswood joined the legion of war widows raising her only child, Tracey's grandmother, on her own. Anne copied the information for Tracey and Brad said he would get it to her.

The Beauchamp cousin in Montreal said she found a reference to the Culver-Beauchamp marriage in a Montreal Gazette social column. She asked Brad to take her to the library where the newspaper archives were kept. Some foundation or another paid to put all the early editions on microfilm. He took her in the cruiser, extracting her she would call him, and not try to go home alone.

∿

Brad continued west out of town. Morrison, the contractor, lived in the first completed home of a new small subdivision near the village of Pine Grove, a tiny spot on the map.

The highway bypassed it but a narrow, hilly road wound into the village past a dilapidated gas station and grocery store, long since closed. The center of the village held only two schools, two churches and few houses. Quite a lot of building for a hundred people, Brad thought. Maybe the new subdivision would liven the place up. The public school sat on a little hill, surrounded by a chain-link fence. At the bottom of the street stood an old one-story store built some time in the 1800's. Brad parked in front.

The interior was a surprise with a general store feel, but the merchandise had gone uptown. The young man at the counter looked uptown as well. He wore a casual open-necked shirt of some silky taupe material with a pair of neatly pressed jeans and the kind of shoes advertised in glossy magazines.

"Can I help you?" he said with a friendly grin.

"Yeah. I'm Brad Compton, Culver's Mills Police. Do you know where the Shining Lake subdivision is?"

"Sure. I hope there isn't any trouble?"

"Not that I know. Were you expecting trouble?"

Brad watched the other man closely. Perhaps he was an ordinarily anxious guy.

"When the cops turn up, I always expect trouble."

"Lots of experience with us, have you?"

"Hey, no, officer. I'm only fooling around. What trouble could there be on a little construction site in the middle of the country?"

"I don't know. I need to talk to a guy called Jake Morrison."

"Jake. Yeah, he's the boss."

Brad noticed the worried lines around the man's face and the sudden ageing. Perhaps he wasn't so young after all.

"Friend of yours, is he?"

"Look, officer. I'm Jake's brother. Name's Ted. I don't want him to have any problems. He has enough with the building and his crazy crew."

"What sort of trouble?"

"Ask him. I don't know anything about it."

From the look on his face, Brad knew that was the last he was going to find out here.

"How do I get there?"

"Left across the bridge, through the rock cut and turn left at the old rail bed road."

"Thanks."

As he pulled away, Brad saw the man's hand reaching for the phone. Morrison would know he was coming, he thought.

The road through the rock cut had been made and paved when the spur rail-road to this area shut down. The narrow track fell away steeply on both sides. It followed a causeway separating the lake from a swampy area, known locally as Grass Lake. On the other side of the causeway, it left the rail bed and followed the shore of the lake closely.

A white clapboard church and steeple stood on the other side of the lake in the village. A road sign pointed the way to the Shining Lake Subdivision-- one completed house and half a dozen others framed in but not roofed as yet. The one completed house should be Morrison's.

A broad expanse of lawn dotted with cedars shaped into balls and spires separated the house from the lake. Large grey stones of the local granite buttressed the shoreline. A power boat, large for this lake, was tied to the floating dock, beside the boathouse. A man ran towards it.

"Hey, Morrison. Stop. I want to talk to you."

A powerful roar from the engine was his only response.

A dog yapped at the screen door when Brad came up to the house. A slight woman, Chinese or maybe Vietnamese with dark hair pulled back in a ponytail stared out at him with frightened eyes. Brad held his identification up to the door.

"Rusty, be quiet," she said to the Jack Russell terrier at her heels. "What do you want?"

"I need to talk to Jake Morrison. I'm Brad Compton with the Culver's Mills police. And you are?"

"Denise Morrison. Jake left. What do you want with him? He's not in any trouble, is he? Why can't he be left alone?"

The words tumbled out of her with no space left between for Brad to answer. One of her hands clasped the door frame so tightly the fingers were white. Finally, she stopped. Not to breathe. She seemed to hold her breath. So still he wasn't sure she was aware of him.

Brad spoke as quietly as he would have to a child or a frightened animal. "Mrs. Morrison, I want to ask him a question. He's not in any trouble that I know."

"What's the matter?"

"Nothing is the matter. He's not here. Go away. Go away now."

She continued to stare past Brad, watching the lake, or nothing.

"When will he be back?"

"I don't know!"

The heavy patio door closed, cutting off the sound of her voice. She pulled the heavy drapes across.

Brad walked down to the water. Nothing to be seen on the lake in either direction. Nothing doing on the construction site either. He walked back to the car. He'd better go back to town and work on the land deals. Adam wouldn't be too happy he had gone out alone.

Around the bend in the shoreline, the big boat drifted slowly about its anchor. Jake Morrison, a tall, sandy-haired man waited. From time to time he took off his baseball cap and wiped his balding head. Finally, he heard the sound of an engine. He'd better risk it. It wouldn't be good to leave her alone too much longer, the shape she was in these days. Damn that Smith woman anyway. Why hadn't she left them alone? And now the cops, pushing and prodding and leaving her a hysterical mess, no doubt.

As he tied up at the dock, he watched the house. There was only a little movement at the drape over the patio door. Was it Denise watching him or the big cop? As he neared the door, the drape flew back, and Denise ran out the door and across the stones of the patio to him.

"Oh, Jake, I was so scared. What did he want? What is the matter? We have to go away from here. What have they found out? Soon they'll come to take me away."

Jake held her against him until the trembling had stopped.

"Nothing about you, pet. Nothing about you. It's sure to be about those land deals the woman was hounding me about. She's dead. She didn't know about you. It's not about you."

His soothing voice whispered on and on in her ear.

"Come in the house and make us some tea. You know that makes you feel better."

"Yes, a nice cup of tea."

When Brad left her and her young policewoman guard at the library, Anne climbed the stairs to the stone and glass addition housing the reference library and a small art gallery which elbowed out from the rear of the old building. The guard stayed in the hall to watch the stairs and the elevator. Anne passed by the door of the gallery. There were so many things she had wanted to do on this visit. The gallery contained some interesting old portraits, painted by itinerant artists early in the last century and a collection of works by local artists.

Stacks of old reference books at one end and computer terminals at the other bracketed the long reference room. In between stood square oak tables worn with use. Anne loved to work in reference libraries, with room to spread out and interested people to help. The reference librarian, a thin, pleasant blonde woman named Mrs. Wolfe, assisted her in setting up the viewer and finding the correct roll of film.

She had searched back three decades when the librarian tapped her on the shoulder.

"It's 5:00 pm, Dr. McPhail. If you want to work longer, you can. Turn off the machine and the lights when you go. You have to leave by eight o'clock, though."

"I had no idea it was so late. Thanks so much for your help."

Anne stood up and stretched as Mrs. Wolfe leave. She thought she would look through a few more years of records before calling Brad.

She had to keep reminding herself to stick to the social items. The histories, politics, even advertisements of the day were fascinating.

Ads appeared for long ago trades. Hat makers were prominent. It was, however, in a small column beside an advertisement for Wm. Goodwin, painter, that she found the long-lost couple, in a simple announcement that the marriage had taken place. Such hurried marriages usually meant that a baby was coming a little early, so she went ahead six months and looked for births. Intent as she was, she was startled to hear the door of the room open and close again, and heavy footsteps across the carpet. She sat, still and frightened, in front of the view screen.

"Anne, what's the matter?"

She turned and reached a hand to Brad.

"I'm so glad to see you. I lost track of time, and you startled me. I thought you were the killer, coming to get me."

Her voice was unsteady.

"I should have called out from the door. I'm sorry. The guard was outside, until now."

"I forgot. I was so intent because I had found the marriage and I was looking for the baby."

"Baby?"

"I think there must have been a pregnancy; the marriage seemed so low-key. There was no celebration, just an announcement."

"Can you put the books away, because I have to take you home now? It's almost eight o'clock."

Anne swiveled to look at the clock. Almost eight o'clock. She had promised to be home for dinner at seven. She gathered up her belongings but left the books where they were. She scribbled a brief note asking Mrs. Wolfe to leave them for her return.

Catherine and her sons were finishing dinner when she arrived. She had saved Anne a portion of chicken fricassee with dumplings. Anne apologized as she sat down to eat.

"I'm so sorry I was late, Catherine. I was working at the library and lost track of time until Brad came to get me."

"Any luck at all today?" Catherine asked as she served salad to her.

"I found the record for a marriage I was looking for, and now I need to find a birth record. It does all seem remote from today and these awful murders. Let's talk about something else. Gardening for example."

They had a lot to talk about with the spring gardening season just beginning. Anne's garden at home was still snow-covered or had been when she left. It was a gardening zone or two cooler than Catherine's. Catherine focused on vegetables and herbs for her kitchen, with raised beds behind the house. She did have some flower beds and especially a cutting garden, as she liked to have flowers in the rooms when the guests came.

Anne described her home on a Northern lake. The lawn behind the house sloped down to a stone breakwater. She had developed several rose gardens near the house, mostly the tougher Canadian Explorer roses. Against her grey stone home, she grew a William Baffin climber, covered with strawberry-pink blossoms in the spring. By the time they had got this far, Anne was ready for bed and said good night.

Chapter Seventeen

I t was only 5am when Adam pulled on his jogging clothes and started out for a run. Not yet dawn. He talked to his advisor after class about the possibility of taking his law degree full-time.

He started taking classes to help him be a better policeman, but he had to decide if he wanted to go one further, complete the degree and change careers.

He enjoyed his present work, but with a degree, he would have a lot more choice; the FBI if he wanted to stay in law enforcement or the Attorney General's department, a practice in one of the many large firms, legal or otherwise, if he didn't. Recently, he had a feeling he was marking time, but he put that down to more personal matters: no wife, no family, and the essential loneliness of his life.

He stopped at the weir where mist rose from the open river below.

What about Erin? He really liked her, and he thought she liked him. He worried his job might come between them. A safe job might appeal to her more, or was he projecting his own doubts onto her?

HIs route took him past Erin's shop, but he didn't stop.

And what about money? He had enough saved to do a year of, but it would leave him with no savings at all. This dreary thought found him in front of his little house. At least it was rented. He could turn the key and move to Burlington at any time or commute. Sam was waiting for him inside, indignant at the lack of food in her dish.

After he had showered and shaved, Adam checked in at the station on his way to interview Ada Warren. Pete had the address of the owner of a grey Camaro who had been released from jail that week Assault with a deadly weapon. Pete had gone to check him out. Anne was going back to the library when it opened.

Brad was at the computer but followed Adam to his office door. He had a hangdog look on his normally cheerful face.

"What's up?"

Brad quickly told him the story of his visit to the lake.

"Dammit. What if you had run into trouble? No backup, no one even knowing where you were."

"I know, boss. I'm sorry. It won't happen again."

"Okay. I'm going over to Ada's. You sniff around a bit. See what you hear about Morrison."

Adam liked the old neighborhood around Ada's home. The houses were small and well cared for. He found Ada working on her front garden. She seemed to be raking mounds of rotting material off the beds.

"What are you doing, Ada?"

"Pulling the mulch from the beds."

"What's it for?"

"It protects the plants from heaving out of the ground during thaws in the winter, and the ground from thawing too soon when there is still a danger of frost in spring," she said. "I doubt you came for here for gardening information. Come inside and have a coffee with me. I need a warm-up."

Adam followed the vigorous old lady into her kitchen. Sometime in the past, it had been expanded to make room for a fireplace, comfortable sofa, and a table and chairs. Adam sat in front of the fireplace as Ada poured their coffee.

"You're right. I want to ask you about some gossip."

"Gossip?"

"Old gossip. Anything you might have heard when you were very young of a scandalous nature about the Culvers or the Beauchamps."

"Why on earth—"

"We're trying to get a handle on Jennifer's blackmailing activities."

"It's hard to believe any Beauchamp could be blackmailed. That hard-headed bunch wouldn't take that from anyone. Publish and be damned would be their attitude, each and every one of them." Ada shook her head at him emphatically.

"That's what Thomas Beauchamp said too."

"He would."

"What about the Culvers?"

"They're a different story. Very proud and quite determined their line is

89

pure aristocrat back to Revolutionary times. David Culver is particularly touchy on the subject. One day in class I suggested many families in this part of the world had some Native American in their background, and the further back a family went the more likely it became. He was almost apoplectic, and he was only fifteen years old."

"Who does the attitude come from?"

"Naomi, I think. She's a New York Armstead herself. She wrote me a stiff note the next day. Either she took it as a personal affront, or she wanted to protect David."

"Why?"

"Lord knows. Maybe they do have something to hide."

"Have you heard anything like that, specifically about them?"

Ada shook her head. "No, but I'd have Anne McPhail looking if I were you."

"The whole town knows she's helping me?"

"Yes, indeed."

Adam thanked her and left. When he reached his car, the phone was ringing.

"Pete. You'd better come over to this guy's place. Someone beat me to him."

"Where are you?"

"Eighty-seven Arthur Street, in the back."

Eighty-seven Arthur Street was a dump. Ramshackle was too kind a word for it, with its almost non-existent paint, a yard full of car parts and tires, and a porch barely hanging onto the front wall.

Pete called down the stairs as he came in the front door, "Up here, Adam."

The body hung on the windowsill, at the end of a trail of blood that started inside the door. An exit wound gaped through the hole in a pale blue shirt. The contents had been dumped from a battered dresser, and the door to the closet stood open. The room smelled of blood and dirty clothes.

"Looks like he interrupted someone tossing his room," Pete said.

"Is this the guy you were after?"

"Yeah, Dave Lauder. I knew him. The grey Mazda out in front is registered to him. He renewed the plate when he got out of prison. He was a small-time crook working his way up. Assault with a deadly was the last."

"Who was his lawyer?"

"Don't know. I'll check the court records."

They worked on with the crew they shared with the county for forensics. By the end of the afternoon, they were no further ahead, except for many different fingerprints.

When Adam came into the squad room, Anne met him with a huge grin.

"I found the Culver baby and the descendants."

"Who are they?"

"Your friend, Peg, and her sister, May."

"You're kidding. I never heard they were Culver relations. How did you find out?"

Anne was pleased. Not "are you sure?" but "how did you find out?"

"The Culver baby was a girl, Mary, born at seven months into the parents' marriage in 1917. She had no school record in Culver's Mills. An obituary of the grandmother mentioned a granddaughter, Mary, living in New York City."

"How did you find the obit?"

"The librarian's mother keeps cuttings of obituaries and pastes them into a keepsake book. You know a lot of people in the last generation did the same. My mother keeps hers in a pickle jar."

Anne took a breath and looked poised to continue on the subject of storing obituaries.

"Anne."

"Sorry. Both parents had died of influenza in 1919. I found her marriage to David Jenkins, of New York City in 1937. The trail is cold here in Culvers Mills, but Vital Statistics lists two daughters. Peg married Ian Watson in 1970. May married a man called Peterson in 1964. Neither have children. I don't know how they ended up back in Culver's Mills. "

"You know, the Beauchamps told me their wills were always carefully written. Do you suppose the same is true of the Culvers?"

"This child, Mary, might have inherited something from both sides. I bet Peg Watson doesn't know she's their cousin."

"Can you find out about old wills?"

"They're public record if they haven't been lost or destroyed by fire. Fire took a lot of records in the old days."

"What relation are Peg Watson and Thomas Beauchamp?"

"Second cousins. She's a cousin to the Culvers too."

"I wonder how Leticia's father left his money and land?"

"I suspect a trust fund for a few generations, for the girls. That's how it was usually done. The boys got their money and property when they came of age."

"Could you find out for me?"

"I can try."

"Thanks. I have to tell you there's been another murder."

"Oh no. Who?"

"A man called Dave Lauder. We think he was the one who shot at us."

"Another murder. Why was he killed? Do you know?"

"Someone tidying up, maybe. We are looking for connections with the other victims. I have to go. Are you okay?"

"Sure, fine," said Anne, a little shakily.

Adam left, intending to put off talking to Peg until he had more information about wills and trusts and bloodlines.

Chapter Eighteen

April rain, steady, not too cold, washed away the dirt from the gutters on Friday. The grey morning matched Adam's mood. The case was eight days old; they had had two more murders and two attempts. The Burlington press was starting to nose around, well, more than nose around, and he didn't have a suspect yet.

Pete was making a house-to-house around the latest killing, and Bill Perkins was doing the same in Greenbank. Whoever this medium guy was, he sure blended into the woodwork.

Brad was in traffic court and wouldn't make any progress on the Morrison connection. Anne worked on her own research at the library.

The yellow police tape and the curious had disappeared from the library a few days ago. It was business as usual in the adult section: a few retirees, reading the morning newspapers in the comfortable chairs near the magazine racks, two or three students staring into the computer screens and an animated lady talking fiction with the librarian at the desk. A shy-looking teenage girl, likely a co-op placement, checked books in and out. He stopped to ask where he might find the genealogy reference section and the student directed through a door to the new addition.

Anne's bored-looking minder, Dave, lounged outside the door, straightening when Adam appeared.

"She's inside, Lieutenant."

"How's it going?"

"Looks like dull work to me, but she can keep at it for hours."

Adam found Anne in front of a microfilm reader watching a dizzying progression of names on a census or tax roll or something.

"Morning, Anne. Sorry to interrupt you."

"Not at all. I take frequent breaks, or I'll lose my excellent breakfast. How can I help you this morning?"

"First you can tell me if Brad or Pete drove you here?"

"Yes, Brad did, before court. And Dave met us here. Don't worry. I'm not so foolish as to go out alone."

At least not yet, she thought, knowing how restless she was.

"Okay. Did you find anything after I left yesterday?"

"Not yesterday, but today I found details of Pierre Beauchamp's will. He was a wealthy man with railroad interests, banks and land. He left his major business interests to his son and a large trust with money and land investments for his daughters and their offspring. The only ones still living and benefiting from the trust are the descendants of Isabelle, the youngest daughter. Her family lived in New York. There are about 5 cousins who share a substantial income that would, of course, be smaller if divided seven ways. I don't understand how Peg and May became excluded. Their grandmother Leticia was the beneficiary of an irrevocable trust, and even if her father was angry with her, she couldn't have been cut out."

"Who were the trustees?"

Adam smiled. She hadn't been able to leave it alone.

"His son, his lawyer, and his man-of-affairs sort of an accountant or business manager."

"Could they have arranged to forget this troublesome little cousin, if they had tried?"

"I suppose so."

Anne was doubtful, but Adam knew trustees often had enormous power. He needed to talk to Peg Watson, and not at her lunch counter. He phoned and asked her if he could visit her at her home on business.

Peg lived on a quiet street in the older part of town. Her house sat back from the street, with a white picket fence surrounding a tidy front lawn. It looked cared-for but not the home of a woman receiving a significant income from a trust fund.

Peg offered him coffee, and they sat drinking it in her large blue and white kitchen. Adam began to tell her the story of their investigations.

"Anne McPhail has been working on the Beauchamp genealogy, and she found something that concerns you and your sister."

"Concerns us? We have nothing to do with the Beauchamps."

"Do you know anything about your own family?"

"Not a lot. My mother died when I was only one and May, you know my sister, May?"

Adam nodded, and Peg went on. "May was only three. Our dad and Granny Jenkins raised us. In fact, they never said much about my mother, and I never asked after the first few times. They were both so upset because she was murdered."

"Murdered?"

"Yes, gunned down outside our apartment. The police thought she was an innocent victim of some kind of gang violence. It happened in New York City in those days, too."

"Did you get the impression your father disliked your mother's family?"

"All he ever said was they would have nothing to do with us, and that suited him just fine."

Adam told her what Anne found.

"If you're Leticia Beauchamp's granddaughters, you should be getting a large income from the grandfather's trust."

"But why wouldn't the trustees make sure my grandmother and grandfather knew?"

"Maybe they didn't want to share the wealth. I'm going out to have another talk with Thomas Beauchamp who is one of the current trustees. The other two are trust officers of a bank, so once you produce your identification and your mother's I am sure they will see you get what you are entitled to."

"Adam, I'm overwhelmed. My sister has a chronic arthritis, and this will make such a difference for us. I'm so grateful to you."

Adam smiled but shook his head. "Not to me. To Anne McPhail. She did all the work. And your great-grandfather wanted you taken care of. If you have any trouble with getting documents for your mother, I'm certain Anne will help you."

Peg gave him an impulsive hug at the door. It wasn't often a policeman got to deliver good news. He was cheered up all the way to his vehicle. Now for Thomas Beauchamp and the redoubtable Andrea.

Chapter Nineteen

t the Beauchamp home, cleaners' trucks, painters, and a furniture van all suggested a major undertaking. The young maid opened the door.

"Good morning, Tracey. Is Mr. Beauchamp at home today?"

"Yes, but he's busy."

"He'll see me. Tell him I need to talk about the Beauchamp Family Trust Fund."

She bustled away to the library.

"Mr. Davidson, do you usually announce private business to the maid who opens the door?"

"Only when I'm being stonewalled, Mr. Beauchamp. Where can we talk?"

In the library, the florid-faced Beauchamp confronted Adam. "What do you mean by all this?"

"Mr. Beauchamp, you told me Beauchamp wills were always water-tight, so you didn't care whatever Jennifer turned up. Are you sticking to that?"

"Of course, I am."

"What about Leticia Beauchamp Culver's descendants and the fact they haven't received one red cent from the trust set up for them?"

A perplexed look came over Beauchamps' face as he sat down in the nearest chair.

"Leticia and Douglas didn't have any children, as far as I know," he said.

"They had a daughter, Mary, born seven months after they were married. A distant cousin in New York raised her after her parents died. She died young, and her husband lost touch or was ignored by the family here. There are two granddaughters, one of them ill. The other is an honest, hard-working person.

"Are you sure? Do these people have documentation?"

"These people have no idea about any of it. We found it in the course of our investigation. And yes, it is well documented."

"I'll call my mother."

When Andrea Beauchamp appeared, she hurried to her son's side, alarmed by his pallor.

"What have you been bullying Thomas about?"

Thomas reached out a hand to stop her angry tirade. "Mother, do you know anything about a child called Mary, of Leticia and Douglas Culver."

"Of course. She died in New York City."

"Did you know she had children?"

"No, I didn't. She was always angry with the family for sending her away after her parents died."

"Why was she sent away, Mrs. Beauchamp?" Adam said.

He knew Anne would want to know.

"I think my mother-in-law was embarrassed by the circumstances of her birth—she was a seven-month baby, you know—and my mother-in-law was a ferocious and unkind old Victorian.

"To your knowledge, was a deliberate attempt made to deny her share of the trust?"

"No. Certainly not. Did she have children?"

"Yes, ma'am. Two daughters."

"Thomas, you're the trustee. You must check all this and, if true, do what is right for those girls."

The old lady stood up in her dignified manner and held out a hand.

"Thank you, Mr. Davidson. We will look after them."

"Mrs. Beauchamp, Jennifer Smith never said anything about this to you?"

"Not a word."

Adam had to be content with that. On the whole, he believed them, unless he found some kind of evidence they did know or had been paying blackmail. He paused at the front door to let the painters pass through.

"What's going on here, Tracey?"

"Claire Beauchamp is getting married next month."

On the way back into town, Adam thought about whether or not he should speak to Peg before the lawyers. It would be better if he told her first, he concluded.

Lunchtime filled the diner, but Adam found a place at the counter. As Peg cleared the dishes and wiped up in front of him, he told her she should contact Thomas Beauchamp with her documents. When she seemed hesitant, he assured her that, if not welcoming, they would at least be polite. Much later Peg told him they welcomed her and her sister warmly.

After the chicken potpie, Adam called Pete to meet him at Bill Perkins office.

In Owen, a medium-sized town southwest of Culver's Mills, the municipal building, newly-built in the 50's, with glass and colored panels decorating the facade, housed the county sheriff's office. Sheriff Perkins and Pete had their feet up among the remains of coffee and sandwiches on the desk.

They spent the afternoon reviewing and correlating the evidence, including good physical evidence. The files in Davis' office contained legal business. The search of Davis's home by Perkins' men revealed bank accounts with money transfers out of the country to the Cayman Islands, but they were only thousands, not millions. The house-to-house inquiries didn't turn up much either. Davis had been dead about twenty-four hours but other than the black SUV and the nondescript stranger, they had no new leads. Bill hadn't heard anything about Morrison either.

Adam crashed his boots to the floor in disgust. "Let's go, Pete. It looks like we're back to those damn files and genealogy charts."

In Culver's Mills, lights in the square glowed through the darkness of the late afternoon rainstorm. The windows of Erin's shop darkened as he passed and the sign turned from open to closed. He wheeled into the space in front. He could see Erin's silhouette at the back of the shop and tapped on her door window.

"Hi, Adam. Come in," she said to him when she unlocked the door. "Would you like some coffee or tea or a drink?"

"I'd love a beer if you have any. I'm coffee-ed out."

"In the office all day?"

"Bill Perkins, the sheriff's office. Worst coffee in the county. We went over the details of this case."

He took the beer and sat back in a wing back chair, with a contented sigh as he stretched out his legs towards the fire.

"What happened to the art deco chairs?"

Erin had changed the whole grouping again.

"A couple from Toronto came in and bought the lot. They said deco is popular up there right now."

Adam spent the next few minutes telling her how much he enjoyed their evening together. The more time he spent with her, the more he liked her and the more relaxed he felt. He found himself telling her about his law classes and his advisor's talk with him.

"Could you quit police work, Adam?"

"I think so. I haven't done a lot of different things, but I'm not one of those guys who say being a cop is who I am. For me, it's what I do now. I enjoy the disciplined thinking of the law."

"It's a tough decision."

"I have a little while."

He waved the decision away.

"What did you decide about the cast party after the play tomorrow night. Would you like to come?"

"I'd like to, but would the others be uncomfortable with me there?"

"They'll have to lump it. I'll leave you a ticket at the front."

Adam stood up to go. Erin moved into his arms, hugged him and put her face up to be kissed.

They both spoke at once.

"See you soon."

The next morning, Brad's lanky form hunched over the keyboard. When he saw Adam, he bounded across the room.

"I've got him."

D. Calvert was a passenger on a ship out of Liverpool. Anne said that Calvert was the original name for the Culvers. He showed him the printout of the passenger list. The date and month matched the entry against D.C. in Jennifer's file. He appeared against several entries of $3,000 each. Time to have a word with Mr. David Culver. Brad deserved to be in on this interview, so they drove together out to the estate.

Adam didn't know the maid who opened the door. When he asked where Mrs. Ames was, the maid told him she left on a short vacation. Perhaps Mrs. Ames decided whatever she wanted to say to him wasn't important after all.

Culver appeared, blustering as usual, with his narrow face even more pinched with the strain.

"What are you here for?"

You'd think he'd at least try to be polite, Adam thought.

"Mr. Culver, we'd like to know why you didn't tell us Jennifer Smith was blackmailing you?"

The young man sat down, all bluster gone, as his grandmother entered the room.

"David, what are they talking about?"

He made a few vague noises and waved his hand at Adam.

"We have evidence David, among others, was paying Jennifer Smith a large sum of money, in his case, monthly. As you can see by looking at him, ma'am, it's true."

"David?"

The warning note in his mother's voice was unmistakable.

"Mother, she knew about the indian."

"What indian?"

"The one they say was involved with great-great-great-grandfather. She was going to announce we were aboriginal."

There had to be more to it than that, Adam thought.

"You paid that woman money to keep that secret?"

His mother was incredulous.

"But you always were so proud of our French heritage."

"David, I knew you had some foolish ideas, but this is too much. Because some remote ancestor had a liaison with an aboriginal does not change our family history."

"I only wanted to save us embarrassment. Now it will all come out."

He was holding his head in his hands.

"Mr. Culver, if all you did was pay blackmail, then you're the victim here. We won't have to tell anyone unless it is evidence in a murder trial."

"Murder. No. I didn't kill her."

The plaintive tone changed to panic.

"How about you give us details of the blackmail scheme?"

The frightened young man explained Jennifer's technique. She advertised her genealogical services to the local paper and elsewhere. For his grandmother, David asked her to develop a family tree. She met him for lunch in Burlington, and she picked up on his extreme pride in family and distaste for anything that sullied their pure line.

When she was unable to find evidence of a second and parallel family, she went further back and found an aboriginal connection. She made it clear she would make sure the community knew unless he paid. He met her once a month in Burlington and handed over the cash. He'd paid her for three months before she was killed.

"I didn't kill her, Lieutenant. I was with my family that night. I didn't go out again after we got home. I didn't meet her at the library, only in Burlington."

"We'll need your DNA and fingerprints. You should also know our researcher hasn't found any such connection for your family."

"You mean she made it up?"

"Sure, why not. She could fake a family tree if you didn't ask to see original documents."

"I can't believe I was such a fool."

After a pause, as David sat and stared alternately at the floor and at his grandmother, Adam said, "When were you last in the library?"

"Not for about a year. I was on the fund-raising committee for the addition, but I haven't been in since we opened it."

"Then you have no worries. Come with us and give us a statement and samples, and I won't have to bother you again."

Adam watched the worried glances from grandmother to grandson. Finally, David straightened. "I'll come with you, Lieutenant."

Brad and Adam took Culver to the cruiser. He was calmer now and hugged his grandmother, assuring her he did nothing wrong. He was quiet and thoughtful on the way to the courthouse where his lawyer met them. Adam treated Culver as a victim witness, except to take the samples. David insisted on giving the samples over his lawyer's objections.

Brad was upset when Culver left. All that work for nothing. A few choice phrases expressed his feelings.

"You know, you've cleared away most of the underbrush from this case. We've eliminated several major suspects."

"Yeah, but what are we left with?"

"Maybe someone who had money to lose. Not indian ancestors or lost cousins, but a lot of money. Someone paid her $8,000 a week."

"There is nothing about $8,000 in any of her files."

"It has to be something she found in her research. What about Davis? Did you find anything in his files?"

"Perkins hasn't passed them over yet. I'm supposed to get them tomorrow. You and Pete both looked at them, didn't you?"

"Yes, but as far as I could tell it was ordinary business, some real estate deals, minor criminal stuff, traffic court. He was Dave Lauder's attorney on a couple of charges, so that may have been the connection. He could have hired Lauder to hit Jennifer and then Anne."

"I don't know. Lauder was small time assault. He may have fired the shot at Anne, but I don't see him as the murderer."

Adam grunted.

"Let's call it a day."

Atkins watched David Culver walk down the steps of the courthouse and drive off with his lawyer. He didn't look like a guy under arrest, the reporter thought, as he pushed his way through the heavy door of the police station.

"Lieutenant, have you arrested Culver?" he said, interrupting the intense conversation in the squad room.

"Mr. Culver has been helpful. He is not under arrest. Next time call ahead."

Adam brushed past Atkins and disappeared out the door.

"Whew, that's not like him. What's going on?"

"You'll have to ask the lieutenant. I'm out of here," Brad said

Atkins stood in the middle of the squad room, meeting the amused gaze of the receptionist.

"Must have been a bad day," he said, as he left the office, banging the door in disgust behind him.

Adam picked up Anne at the library and dropped her at Catherine's. She thought she was close to finding the disputed land record of long ago. Adam told her about the Beauchamps and the Culvers.

"So much pain for such foolish reasons. What's past is past."

"I'm surprised to hear you say so when you are so keen on this ancestor stuff."

They were sitting in Catherine's driveway, watching the first rays of sun of the day, and the last, play across her yard. The rain had stopped.

"I'm interested and curious, but whatever I learn doesn't change who I am and what I have done. Good night, Adam."

"Good night."

Chapter Twenty

The next morning was bright and cheerful, but Anne's mood wasn't. She spent one of those too-early mornings brooding about the events of the last few days. Two attempts on her life were too much. She wanted to go home. Canada would be a lot safer.

Even as she thought this, Anne realized she didn't want to leave without knowing the solution to the murder or without getting the information she wanted for her own family research. Perhaps she could visit one or two of the local churches to check their records today. Then she would go.

She showered in the bathroom attached to her bedroom and dressed for a walk in slacks, a pullover and her favorite wool socks.

"Good morning, Anne. Coffee?

Catherine set freshly-baked biscuits and her own strawberry jam out on the table.

"Yes, please."

"Do you have plans for today?" Catherine asked.

"I thought I might visit one or two local churches looking for my great-great great-grandmother's marriage record."

"Which churches are you going to visit?"

Catherine put mugs on the table and sat opposite Anne.

"There's a Catholic church here?" said Anne.

"Oh, yes, on the other side of the river from here."

"What about Anglican?"

"Anglican—they call it Episcopalian here. It's off the square. Why do you think those two?"

"My great-great-great-grandfather was French-Canadian so most likely Catholic but there were proselytizing Anglican priests who came through here also."

"I'm sure Margaret Kennedy, the secretary at the Catholic Church, will help you. Would you like me to drive you over?"

Anne's car had been demolished, the frame twisted beyond repair in the accident.

"No thanks. I'm going to the car rental place and get something I can drive home."

"Are you leaving soon?"

"I'm not sure. Is it okay if I stay a few more days?"

"Of course. Didn't Adam want you to go on taking precautions?"

"I can't do that forever, Catherine. He may never find the killer."

Catherine reached for a note beside the phone on the counter.

"You had a phone call, from a reporter from the paper. He's called Ted Atkins. I told him I would give you the message."

"I don't like to talk to the press. You never know how your words will come out."

"I don't think you have to. Refer him to Adam."

After breakfast, Anne walked through the sunshine to the car rental agency and picked out the safest sedan she could find. The clerk gave her directions to the Catholic Church.

St. Mary's was a small, quite old, stone church, set in a well-tended graveyard, its wrought-iron picket fence shining with a new application of paint. A team of roofers was replacing shingles. Either the congregation was more significant than the church looked, or more affluent, she thought.

The church office was in the back. A door to the right led to a hall full of seniors taking clogging lessons. The clack of their heels echoed in the hallway as Anne knocked at the office door.

"Come in."

Not Margaret Kennedy, a man's voice.

"Oh, good morning," Anne said. "I'm looking for Mrs. Kennedy."

"I'm Father O'Brien," the elderly man behind the desk introduced himself. "Margaret is away today. Can I help you?"

"I'm Anne McPhail. I've come to Culver's Mills to research my genealogy, and I wondered if I could search your oldest records if you have any?"

Father O'Brien stood up, not very far for he was a remarkably short individual, not more than five feet tall.

"We do have some records from the turn of the eighteenth century—baptismal and marriage records. We keep them in the back of the church."

"In a regular room, Father?"

Anne was horrified. Paper deteriorated rapidly in today's atmosphere.

"No, no, Ms. McPhail."

The little priest was equally horrified.

"Doctor McPhail, Father," Anne said. "I'm a pediatrician, and this searching the past has become my hobby."

"Indeed. I'm sure you must find it interesting. We were fortunate enough to be given money to outfit and air-condition a small room to hold all our old records."

He led her further down the hall to a surprising room, tiny but newly dry-walled and painted. Humidity monitors and thermostats automatically controlled the temperature and moisture content of the air. The old parish record books, covered in impossibly old cracked leather, lay on Mylar covered shelves. Someone knowledgeable advised them, Anne thought.

"Many of these have been transcribed to cd-rom," he said.

"The gift must have been very generous," Anne said.

"Yes, it was, and anonymous." The priest shook his head. "I can't pray for her by name."

"You're sure it was a woman?"

"Not sure, but I feel it most likely was. Now, what should we be looking at?"

"The baptism was in 1778, so we should look for a marriage fifteen or more years later."

"1793 or so. Those are not transcribed as yet."

He pulled several parish record books from the shelves. On the table were several pairs of white cotton gloves. Anne followed Father O'Brien's lead in pulling on gloves before handling the books. They sat in a comfortable silence, searching for the elusive Margaret through the fragile pages. The writing, in an elegant 18th-century copperplate, was clear after all these years.

Towards lunchtime, Father O'Brien left her, and she could hear the bells ring for a mass. She turned the last page for 1795 when she caught the name de la Ronde. December 31st, 1795. A marriage between Charles de la Ronde and Margaret Pewadguonekwe was celebrated with a mass. Perhaps she could find the children.

As she moved forward through the past, she found the baptism of first one child, then the next. Many times, she had seen records of whole family groups baptized at the same time, after their parents' marriage had been celebrated, sometimes twenty or thirty years after the first child was born. This pair seemed to have lived a more routine life.

On the same page as one of the La Ronde offspring of Charles and Margaret, she noticed the baptismal record of Daniel Beauchamp, godparents Pierre and Madeline Beauchamp, father Michel, and mother, Marie. So the family had remained for a time in Culver's Mills. Anne copied the information into her ever-present notebook and when Father O'Brien returned she asked if she could photograph the page. She assured him she wouldn't use a flash.

When Anne finished, he said, "I'm delighted you found your ancestor, my dear, and that she was a daughter of this church."

"Thank you, Father. I've been following her trail for a long time now. It's so exciting to have an aboriginal ancestor, to have a connection to the country that goes so far back."

"Others would be embarrassed."

"Perhaps. Not an attitude I can easily understand."

Anne stood up and offered her hand to the little priest, who took it in both of his and shook it warmly. Anne dropped a generous donation in the parish box. If they couldn't find enough information on Jennifer's computer, she might have to come back to search the records here. She had a strong suspicion Jennifer was the anonymous donor, although she had no idea how to find out, or if it was even essential to know what she had done with the cash. She drove over to the station to help Brad.

As she walked in the back door of the courthouse, she noticed a man watching her from across the parking lot. When she came in and described him to Adam, he told her the man was likely the reporter, Atkins.

"What does he want with me?"

"He wants to ask you general questions about genealogy research. I told him you wouldn't answer anything else. The Culvers own the paper, and he's worried he'll offend them."

"So much for freedom of the press."

"They're proud and private people."

"If he catches up with me, I'll listen to his questions. That is all I may do, listen."

"Up to you."

Adam spent the morning report writing but sent Brad out to learn what more he could about Morrison. Anne planned to research the Culver lands to see if any parcels belonged to Douglas then forward to find out what had happened to them. Computers made this checking easy. They were lucky both victims had used theirs so extensively.

When they broke for lunch, Brad took Anne to the library and met Adam at Lil's. As they settled into booths, Adam questioned Brad about his morning.

"Did you learn anything about Morrison?"

"I went out to the construction site, but the only guys out there were the framers. They're trying to get the houses closed in, so they weren't much for talking. One fellow said Morrison was usually an okay guy to work for, but lately he had been ugly."

"Ugly?"

"Yeah. Taking something out on the crews. Nothing was ever right. Some of the guys were thinking of quitting, in spite of decent wages."

"Because the boss was hard to get along with?"

"So they said, but I don't think I have the whole story yet. Doesn't explain why Morrison's wife is so wound up either."

"Maybe she's what's on his mind?"

"I can't find anyone who knows her. He's local. His family owned the property he's building on. At least most of it. I think he had to do some deals for some of the shorelines."

"Legit?"

"I doubt it. The brother wasn't too happy about me talking to the crew. He came along and suggested I leave. I didn't think you wanted me to make something of it, at least not yet, so I left."

Brad hesitated, waited for a nod from Adam and went on. "I think we should talk to him. Morrison, not the brother."

"After lunch."

After lunch, they rode out to the worksite where six houses were in various stages of completion. The wind whistled through the gaps left for windows, swirled leaves across the plywood floors, picked up scattered sawdust, and blew it into small piles against the walls. No workers. Not even equipment.

Adam and Brad swung up into the open doorways, crossed from lot to lot. Nothing.

"Let's go visit the lady," Adam said.

Brad backed the car down to the main road and pulled into the lane leading to the Morrison home. Only silence met their repeated knocks on the door, though smoke curled in lazy circles from the chimney.

"Mrs. Morrison. It's Brad Compton, police. We'd like to talk to you."

Silence.

"I'll check the lakefront," Adam said. "Keep on calling to her."

Grass and weeds were taking over most of the flower beds. Maybe the lady was depressed. He could hear Brad calling her first name now. He walked across the terrace to the sliding doors. The drapes weren't entirely pulled.

Something was out of place in the perfect room. Adam realized he was staring at a shoe attached to a foot visible at the corner of the white leather sofa.

"Brad, Brad. Get around here."

He pushed open the sliding door and knelt by the woman on the floor. Alive, but only just, he thought. Pale, clammy skin and shallow breathing. Shock, he thought.

"Call an ambulance. Tell the crew we'll meet them at the rock-cut with the victim. I don't think we have time to get them all the way in here."

He did a quick search of the room while Brad called in. A bottle of Johnny Walker Red whiskey and a glass sat on the big polished slice of a tree trunk that served as a coffee table. He found a pill bottle on the dark green carpet beside it. Ativan. That was some sort of tranquillizer, he thought. No note. They'd come back after they met the ambulance.

Adam picked the tiny woman up and carried her through the front door. Brad sat with her in the back seat, holding her head in a safe position, while Adam slammed the cruiser into reverse and headed out the lane. The road was so rough Brad hugged the woman's body to his to keep her on the seat. Adam made better time after they reached the smoother road over the old railway bed.

The siren of the ambulance wailed as they crossed the causeway, and they saw the flashing lights when they turned the final corner. The crew waited by the open back doors of the ambulance.

"She's still breathing but awful slow," Brad said as they hoisted her out of the back seat and onto a stretcher.

"We've got her, Brad," said one of the paramedics.

"Hey, Mac. Her heart's awful slow too."

They had her hooked to a monitor before Brad was out of the car. The other paramedic wrenched the end from the iv tubing with his teeth as he held the needle in the vein. Mac spoke to the doctor at their base hospital.

Adam leaned against the cruiser, his face impassive as he watched the scene. Long minutes passed while the other two worked, shooting medications into the iv lines as the doctor followed their progress on his monitor at their base. Finally, they loaded her into the ambulance.

Adam walked over to Mac.

"She's stable now, Lieutenant," he answered Adam's unspoken question. "We're taking her to Culver's Mills. Looks like she took a lot of those pills."

"Will she make it?"

"Likely, if the Ativan and alcohol are all she took."

"We'll check the house again," Adam said.

Turning to Brad, he said, "Back to the lake. We'll do another check for pills and a note."

At the property, Brad checked the garage, a miniature of the house, with the same double A-frame construction and enough room for three cars. One was there, a dark green Chevy with mismatched doors, one of them only base painted, and a rusted-out license plate.

Adam circled the house checking the doors and windows. No signs of any disturbance. All the doors except the front and the sliders were locked tight. When Brad joined him, they went in, pulling on gloves.

"Any vehicles?" Adam asked.

"An old clunker, hers likely. I bet Morrison drives something better."

A wall of glass in the living room faced the lake, while the fieldstone fireplace filled the opposite wall. A long piece of unstained cedar formed the mantelpiece.

A tiny oriental woman enveloped in the arms of a tall, muscular blonde man, smiled down at him from a picture on the mantle. Mr. and Mrs., Adam guessed. What had Brad said her name was? Denise. Brad said she was frightened. Of him? Or what?

They found empty end tables, no bookshelves, and no clutter of any kind. A long counter separated the living area from the kitchen. Pale oak cabinets with dark burgundy inserts in the doors hid a tidy collection of dishes and pots and pans. The dishwasher was empty.

A scarlet cover on the bed, embroidered with fanciful birds and flowers struck a vivid and unexpected note in the room. A pane of glass with no mullions took half of one wall, opening the bedroom to the forest and lake beyond.

A spicy odor reminded him of her. He had smelled it when he carried her to the car. Her scent, he guessed and found it on the dressing table in the bathroom. He picked up several different bottles of pills. All had her name on them, some older, all with the same doctor, Kavanagh in Culver's Mills. She tried a lot of things to feel better or to sleep. No note.

On the way back to the station, Adam called the hospital. The woman was in intensive care, ventilated, but expected to recover. No one had been looking for her.

He wanted to talk to Anne, but she hadn't returned from the library.

Chapter Twenty-One

Anne worked for an hour at the library to confirm her information. When Douglas Culver died, he owned a piece of land independent of the family holdings, outside present-day Burlington. Anne couldn't find any record of its transfer or mention in probate. Somehow, the records were lost in time. She and the librarian decided the land belonged to Peg and May.

Maybe Brad could drive her to the land, she thought, as she walked back to the station. She was so tired of being afraid. She had known women, abused women, who lived with this feeling all the time. It was exhausting. She couldn't live this way, even for a little while. Adam would understand.

The station was empty of officers. No one to understand or to ask. On the walk back to Catherine's she contemplated packing and leaving. She could go.

And do what, she asked herself. The anxiety would remain, even across the border. As she walked towards Catherine's the same man who was in the parking lot earlier walked towards her. Fear clutched at her as he approached.

"Dr. McPhail?"

"Yes."

"Ted Atkins, from the local paper. Could I ask you a few questions? Maybe Lieutenant Davidson mentioned I would be around?"

"Yes, he did. You do realize that I can't talk about the investigation, do you?"

God, she sounded so uptight and rude, she thought.

"I know that, but what is this genealogy stuff about?"

"If that is all," Anne said with relief, "come up and sit on the porch for a few minutes and I will show you."

Anne got her computer and showed Ted the program she used and sketched how genealogy research was done.

"Jennifer blackmailed people," he said. "How could that be done?"

"Take my own family. I confirmed that one of my ancestors was aboriginal. There might be someone in my family who found that an offensive notion, to the point of being prepared to pay to keep that secret. Or I might run across information about some other family as I searched, such as evidence of past criminal behavior, or illegitimacy, or bigamy. I've seen instances of all these things."

"All in old records? Where do you access them?"

"Yes. On-line, or in archives or in church records, newspapers, land records, old books. I visited a lot of local libraries. You would be surprised at the documents that people leave to their library."

"And what have you found here in Culver's Mills. Any old scandals?"

"Oh no, Mr. Atkins. Everything that I have done here is information I gathered for the police. You will have to ask them."

The reporter's crooked grin beamed at her. "Okay, Dr. McPhail, thanks for spending time with me."

"When this is over if I am allowed to tell you any more, I will."

When he left, she resumed her internal debate, to stay or to go. By the time she talked herself into staying, she was on the road to Burlington.

The librarian loaned her a detailed county map so finding the parcel of land was easy. The route took her very close to Burlington. She expected farmland but was met by gates and a large developer's sign. Peter Horvath, Inc. Who was Peter Horvath and how was he developing land he didn't own? A construction trailer stood on the property, empty. Strange that a big construction site wasn't working on Saturday. As she pulled off the site and headed back to Culver's Mills, a black Jeep passed her. The sight of one of those made her heart race.

Anne broke a few speed limits on her way back. Usually, she enjoyed driving, but today her attention was divided between watching the road ahead and her rear-view. As she pulled up in front of the courthouse, another SUV entered the square. She waited in her car until he drifted pass, and sprinted for the door, bursting through as Adam came out.

"Anne, where the hell have you been? What happened? Come in and sit down. Brad, get Anne some coffee."

"I went to look at some land that Douglas Culver owned. The librarian and I found the records, and we can't find any transfer to anyone else, so the property should belong to Peg and May."

She stopped to sip the hot coffee that Brad handed to her.

"So?"

Adam was still angry.

"So there's a big development by some guy called Howarth going up on it. How can he be building on land he doesn't own?"

"Maybe you missed the sale record?"

"Someone there drives an SUV, a black one, and followed me again. I couldn't read the license because the plates are caked with mud, but the car, truck, whatever you call those things, is clean."

"What do you think, Adam?" Brad asked. "Would title be clear for this guy if Peg started contesting it?"

"I can't see how. It does make a motive, if Jennifer knew him, if she black-mailed Howarth, if we can place him at the scene. Find out what you can about him, and call the director of land records. I want to know what title is on that land.

"Adam, I think I came across Howarth in Davis's files."

Brad played his fingers across the keyboard, calling up financial records.

"Yeah, here he is. Paid Davis one hundred thousand dollars as a "retainer". Davis's bank account shows forty thousand of that being withdrawn over five weeks as a cash withdrawal."

"Cash. What do you suppose he handed over to Jennifer at those dinners in Burlington?"

"It hangs together, but we have to interview this guy. Like I said, find some information on him. Come on, Anne, I think you need to be back at Catherine's. You've done enough detective work for today."

Chapter Twenty-Two

Anne was looking forward to the weekend when she woke on Saturday morning. She still had her own research to work on. Now that she had traced the paternal side of her family back to 1793, she wanted to begin on the maternal side. A lot of work had been already done by yet another cousin, a missionary priest known as Father Frank in the family, who worked in Saskatchewan. He found a Yorkshire couple who immigrated to Canada in 1820. They were her maternal grandmother's ancestors.

It was the grandfather she wanted to find now. He came to Canada in the great British migration before the First World War to homestead in Saskatchewan. The farm was lost in the thirties when, to use her mother's phrase, "the land blew away."

Anne intended to return to the library to do some more digging. She also wanted to learn more about the Beauchamps and their connection to her family. On-line, she found references to several generations of Beauchamps descended from Daniel, until about 1862, when the last male Beauchamp of the line died in the Civil War. He died bravely too and was awarded a medal posthumously. Surely the Beauchamps would appreciate knowing this, in spite of the aboriginal link.

After a fruitless morning at the library, Anne decided to drive out to the Beauchamps after lunch. As she stopped her car in front of the imposing stone building, she noticed the bright blue door. Imaginative, she thought. She wondered which one of them decided on the paint.

The ringing doorbell brought an unusually sunny Tracy in answer.

"Good morning," she almost sang. "Can I help you?"

"I wonder if I could see Mrs. Beauchamp or someone in the family for a few moments?"

Anne handed Tracy one of her business cards as she spoke. On the back, she had written re Beauchamp genealogy.

"Please come in and wait."

Anne waited in the small foyer that opened into the center hallway of the home. A wide staircase all polished and carved wood, with an oriental carpet runner, rose to a landing. Brilliant dark eyes of a beautiful woman gazed at her from a portrait hanging on the wall above the landing. How lovely she is, Anne thought, with those high cheekbones and dark hair, especially with her pale skin set off by a gown of deep red velvet.

The same lovely face approached her from a door to her right.

"Dr. McPhail?"

"Yes, I have been admiring the portrait. You, I assume?"

Anne smiled and offered her hand.

"Yes, many years ago, now." Mrs. Beauchamp said, turning to look at her younger self after briefly touching Anne's hand. "What can I do for you?"

She turned back to Anne, suspicion clouding those lovely eyes.

"I have been doing genealogical research here, and while looking into my own family, I found references to yours, I think, as well as a connection between the two. I thought you might like to see it."

"Would you be asking anything in return, Doctor?" she asked, pulling back slightly.

"Not at all. I know you must be concerned because of all that has gone on here, but I don't want anything at all. In fact, I almost didn't come because some of the information might upset you."

"Upset me! Why? Oh, do come in here

She led Anne into a library. More of the same dark, carved wood surrounded bookcases fronted with beveled glass doors. High backed eighteenth century armchairs, covered with flame-stitched upholstery sat before a fireplace faced with red brick aged to a pale rose.

Mrs. Beauchamp lowered herself into one, not sitting back, but holding herself upright, ankles together and tucked away under the chair.

"What have you found that might upset me? Does it upset you?"

"Not at all. I have known for some time that one of my own ancestors married an aboriginal woman. The family didn't know exactly where they had lived, because he was a soldier, among other occupations, and of course, early records are scanty. Legend had it they had spent time in Vermont. One of my cousins found evidence, a hint really, that they had been here. Your library and the church records have been helpful."

Anne could see the elderly lady growing restive.

"The reference librarian showed me a small diary, donated to the library when it was first opened. A young French woman, following her soldier-husband, had come here. The diary covered many events, including a scandale," Anne went on, using the French word, "that involved Michel Beauchamp, and his marriage to an aboriginal woman, Marie-Angelique de la Ronde. Later on, I found a baptism of a son, Daniel, whose godparents were your husband's own ancestors. I can't find anyone in the line after 1863 when the last male died in the Civil War. He was a hero, I might add, who was awarded a medal for bravery. I have brought photocopies of all I could, and I have digital pictures of the records at the church, which I can print for you if you would like them."

The maid appeared carrying a tray, which held teacups and a cream-colored Spode teapot. Mismatched teacups, hand-painted, early eighteenth-century design, Anne noted. Mrs. Beauchamp lived with her antiques daily, she thought. No display cases here.

"I would like to see your information," Mrs. Beauchamp said after she had poured the tea. "I assume the diary is in the library?"

"I have it here. Because I was coming out to you, the librarian broke the rules and allowed me to bring it. It is written in old French that I can't read."

"Perhaps I can help you," Mrs. Beauchamp replied, smiling faintly. "I took my degree at the Sorbonne in French. My thesis involved literature of the eighteenth century."

"That would be so helpful," said Anne, digging into her briefcase and pulling out the carefully-wrapped little volume. "This book has such importance, I think it ought to be preserved. The library doesn't have the best facilities for keeping old documents."

"I will discuss it with the librarian."

Mrs. Beauchamp didn't go on but began to read as she sipped her tea.

Anne settled back into her chair after pouring herself another cup, watching the elderly lady become lost in the past. Finally, Mrs. Beauchamp sighed and closed the book, holding it gently on her lap.

"Just as you say, Dr. McPhail, that seems to be the only reference to the de la Ronde connection, although the diary does give a picture of life in those times and the attempts people made to have a civilized life in the wilderness."

"Perhaps you would undertake to translate it for the library."

"Perhaps I shall."

At that moment, a knock on the door-case interrupted them, and Thomas Beauchamp came in. "May I join you, Mother?"

"Of course. Dr. McPhail, my son, Thomas."

As Anne and Thomas shook hands, and Anne met his gaze, she realized that this was not only a powerful and attractive man but also a worried man as well.

"What is wrong, Thomas?"

His mother recognized the worry as well.

"Daniel just called from their hotel in Toronto. They are worried about the baby," he said as he pulled a chair near to his mother and sat down.

"Why?"

"Daniel said the baby has a fever and hasn't been drinking well today. I have Daniel on hold on the phone."

"Daniel and his wife are very young, Dr. McPhail," Mrs. Beauchamp noted. "We worry about them, perhaps too much."

"How old is the baby?" asked Anne.

"Two months."

"Could I help you in any way?"

Anne's manner had changed to her professional calm as she realized that the situation is Toronto was more serious than the family was aware.

"Could you talk to Daniel?"

"Of course."

Once on the phone, Anne asked a few questions.

"Daniel, what is the baby's temperature?"

"Over 103.5."

"And is the baby nursing?"

"Yes, but he only stays on a little while and he has been throwing up."

Anne could hear the panic in the father's voice.

"Has he passed much urine in the past three hours?"

"Only a little."

"Any tears?"

"He hasn't cried much. Doctor, what shall we do?"

"Daniel, what hotel are you at?"

"The Chelsea"

"You are only two blocks from the Hospital for Sick Children. Go downstairs and take a taxi to the hospital. Don't walk. It is too cold. Ask the driver to take you to the emergency entrance. Inside there will be a nurse at the triage desk. Tell her about the fever, the vomiting and the lack of urine. Do you have all that?"

"Yes, thank you. Let me talk to my dad."

Anne passed the phone to Thomas who said, "Call me when you have seen the doctor."

He hung up the phone and turned to Anne.

"Does it sound bad?"

"It could be anything, but likely just a virus he picked up, travelling. The temperature and the lack of urine mean the baby has to be seen right away because of his age."

"Should we go up there?"

"I would say wait until he calls you back. Can you fly from here?"

"Yes, we have a plane. Thank you," he said, taking one of her hands in both of his. "Daniel is my youngest. His mother died when he was twelve, and I worry about him too much."

"I'm so pleased I could help," Anne replied, keeping her voice professional and calm, but conscious of the attraction of the dark eyes that looked into hers. "I should go."

"Could we call you when we hear from Daniel?"

"Certainly. Perhaps you could let the baby's own doctor know what is going on?"

"We will."

Thomas walked Anne out to her car and shook hands, before opening her car door. She glanced in the rear-view mirror. He stood in the doorway, watching.

Chapter Twenty-Three

Catherine tapped on Anne's door. Years of responding to late-night telephone calls meant Anne answered the summons in seconds, wide-awake.

"Yes. Come in."

"Thomas Beauchamp is on the line. He insisted I wake you."

Catherine handed Anne the phone.

"Thank you. I'm glad you did. Good morning, Thomas," she said into the phone.

"Yes, it's a great morning. Daniel called from Toronto. If they hadn't taken the baby when they did, he might have died, so we are all very grateful."

"Did Daniel say what was wrong?"

"A urinary tract infection spread to his blood. He has some kind of abnormality called reflux that will need antibiotics for a long time. Is that safe?" he asked.

"Yes it is, and most of the time prevents the need for surgery."

"That's wonderful to hear. Could you come to lunch with mother and me today?"

"I'd be delighted."

"About 1:00pm. Shall I pick you up? I'll be in town."

"That would be fine, thanks."

Anne expected some resplendent car to arrive, a Cadillac or BMW, but the vehicle stopped in front of the house was a lovingly cared-for, silver,

1992 Honda Prelude. Thomas came to meet her as she walked down the steps.

He gave her an impulsive hug.

"Thank you so much. We're sure you saved our baby."

"Thomas, your son and his wife may have more sense than you give them credit for. I'm happy I could help.

Anne held his arms as she tilted her head back to look up into his eyes.

"Sense?" he said. "I don't know. They are both gifted academics, but they are only twenty-four years old."

Thomas helped her into the low front seat of the Honda.

"This is my favorite car. I've had her since she was new."

"From the look of the body, I don't think you drive it in the winter."

"No, she goes in the garage, up on blocks, shrouded in a dust cover. I visit her on Sundays," he said deadpan, with a slight sideways glance at Anne who struggled but failed to contain her delighted laughter.

Lunch was a great success. Anne, Thomas and his mother finding more in common than a narrowly-averted tragedy spent a convivial two hours in conversation ranging from literature to art and travel. When Thomas left her at Catherine's, it was with a European-style kiss on each cheek and a question—could he call her again?

Chapter Twenty-Four

The cast party after the final performance of the play was on Saturday night. Adam and Erin had plans to meet after the performance. The new director, David Mason, was throwing the party. Adam remembered their interview and wondered how the thin-lipped chiropractor would feel about having him as a guest. At least, to his surprise, he would be able to say he liked the play.

Erin was pink-cheeked and bubbly with the aftermath of the success when he went around to the back of the theatre to pick her up.

When she saw him, she hugged him and said, "Did you like it? Didn't it go well? Wasn't David's direction right on the mark?"

"Yes, yes and yes. Are we ready to go? I think I saw most people leave already."

"Yes, but I turn out the lights and make sure the doors are all locked."

"I'll come round with you."

As they walked around the darkened theatre, Erin talked about the play, and how well all the people had worked together.

"It's sad, but the rehearsals go much better without her. She was so nasty in these last few months. Maybe that's because she was acting out of character. Perhaps she fell into the criminal actions, and couldn't get out."

"I think you are too kind to her. She and Davis ran an extensive operation. It wasn't something you would fall into. It took a lot of planning."

"I suppose you're right. I don't like to think badly of her, especially since she died in such a terrible way."

"Let's have fun, Erin, and leave all this behind for a little while."

With that, they checked the last of the doors and walked out to Adam's ancient car.

David Mason lived a little out of town, in one of the newer estate developments: five acres with most of the trees left in place, a horse barn and paddock and an extensive one story house. Twinkling white lights in the trees lit up the grounds. Other lights disguised as mushrooms and frogs marked the path to the front door.

"I didn't know chiropractors did so well," Erin said.

"He drives a Mercedes too."

The party was going at full bore when they walked in. There was a little stir as some of the cast noticed Adam. The host, however, was all smiles as he came up and air-kissed Erin and shook Adam's hand. Adam was able to praise the play and escape. He got drinks for them, and as Erin mingled and went over details of the play with her friends, he stood on the outside of groups and listened to the gossip.

Word had gone around about Peg Watson and her sister. At least to some extent it had. Many people mixed up the old story about a parallel and illegitimate family with the new information that Peg and May were Beauchamp cousins.

"My dear, how will they handle all that money? They have never moved in polite society," he heard one overdressed and drunk matron hiss to another.

She was one of the teacher's wives, he thought. He wondered what she thought polite meant.

Other groups discussed Jennifer's murder, but the speculation was vague. The Culvers and the Beauchamps weren't talking to the locals, so there didn't seem to be much out about their involvement. Thinking of them, he remembered the message to call Mrs. Ames, the Culver housekeeper. He'd no time to call her back, and come to think of it she hadn't answered the door or been around when he was out to see David Culver.

"Are you mingling, or are you eavesdropping?" Erin teased as she took his arm.

"I'm eavesdropping, although this bunch is getting less coherent by the minute."

"There's some food in the other room. Would you like some, or would you like to get a pizza at my place?"

"What a choice. The food in the other room doesn't stand a chance."

They said goodbye to their hosts to a universal chorus of "don't go yet", and escaped down the long driveway.

At Erin's shop, stained glass shades on a few lamps cast a soft, shadowed glow over the interior. The grouping in front of the fireplace had changed again. This time, he sank onto an over-stuffed Victorian love seat. The footstool in front, with its worn cover, was almost as long as the sofa.

"What do you call this cover on the footstool?"

"Needlepoint."

"I think I saw the same kind of thing at the Beauchamps."

"Mrs. Beauchamp likes Victorian furniture."

Erin brought him a glass of red wine and sat down on the sofa beside him. They talked about the party as they waited for the pizza she had ordered on their way from the Mason's.

"Do you know the Ames woman, who is the housekeeper for the Culvers?" he asked.

"She has only worked out there for a few months, and I don't know where she came from. She's not local, at least not from Culver's Mills."

"Have you seen her around the last few days?"

"She came in the shop, the day of the snowstorm."

Erin described the scene with Mrs. Ames.

Adam groaned. "Dammit, I should have called her back when I got her message."

"Hey, I thought we were going to have a night off from your case."

"You are right," he said. "We have a lot better things to talk about and do."

Adam left Erin's early the next morning, hoping to keep the relationship quiet. Her main street home made this a little difficult. He went home to shower and make peace with his angry little cat.

Chapter Twenty-Five

The blinds on the windows of the station were closed, not even the janitor having arrived when Adam walked in. Brad's battered steel desk in the corner held only his computer. Adam had been hoping for information on Howarth. Disappointed, he pushed open the door to his own office to find a report, titled Howarth, staring at him from his desk.

Peter Howarth moved into local development circles here two years before, spread a lot of money around and surprised most developers by acquiring title to a piece of land that wasn't for sale. The land records wouldn't open until Monday, so Brad was stalled at getting at the paper trail.

When Brad came in, he and Adam talked over a strategy for getting a look at Howarth. Collecting for a children's charity seemed like a good ploy.

Howarth lived in a suburb of Burlington in one of those monster homes that are replacing small suburban houses. The house overwhelmed its tiny lot. Brad and Adam parked in the driveway, and Adam walked up to the door and rang the bell.

A small boy with curly dark hair and dark eyes, opened the door.

"Is your dad home, son?"

"Just a minute."

To Adam's surprise, he closed the door again. A slim, blonde, highly made-up woman with frightened eyes came to the door.

"Can I help you?"

"Ma'am, I'm Lieutenant Adam Davidson of the Culver's Mills Police. I'm collecting for the Boys and Girls Club, and I understand your husband has given generously to other worthy causes." Adam smiled his best, most benign smile at her.

"Please come in," she said.

She led Adam through an immensely tall foyer, with a circular staircase carpeted in white, into an expansive and highly-decorated living room. Matched her makeup, Adam thought.

Howarth stood up as she explained Adam's purpose. Adam stuck out his hand. The man was short, square-built with badly scarred skin, small black eyes and very crooked and stained teeth. A dark brown moustache covered his upper lip.

Howarth shook Adam's hand and asked him in middle European accent what the club did. Adam explained its work with underprivileged youngsters. All the time an ominous feeling he had seen this man before nagged at him. He accepted with fulsome thanks an offer of $1,000 and explained that someone would send him a letter and a pledge card.

Brad stayed outside. He walked over to a black jeep that stood a few feet away and gave the dirt-encrusted license plate a discreet kick. Later he would run the plates. As he walked around the jeep, he saw that it had some recent front-end bodywork. Once they got a warrant, it should be easy to match the black paint to that from Anne's car.

Adam appeared and walked quickly down the walk. His face was grim as he got into the passenger side.

"Let's go, Brad."

"What's up, boss?"

"We need more than you and me. That guy gives me a bad feeling. I'm sure that I have seen his ugly face on a poster or bulletin. We need a picture."

"I got the license. We'll get a picture from the department of motor vehicles.

Usually, Adam enjoyed the drive from Burlington to Culver's Mills. The road ran through forested hills and past the lovely lakes that were the main tourist attractions in this part of Vermont. He barely noticed the greening hills and the white blossoms of the wild plum trees. His mind focused on the pockmarked face of the man he left standing in the over-decorated living room.

Brad accessed the department of motor vehicle records and printed a picture. When it emerged, Adam noted that as usual it only bore a faint resemblance to the original.

"We'll have to fax this to the FBI with a written description. It doesn't look a whole lot like him."

"Do you want me to try immigration or Interpol?"

"Sure, and send it to the RCMP. If he is an illegal, he might be known to them."

Many people slipped through the heavily-wooded border. People smugglers along the St. Lawrence, usually bringing Chinese migrants, sometimes brought in others as well. The RCMP might have a file on the guy.

He should call John Whitfield, the chief of detectives in Burlington to see if he had anything on Howarth. On the other hand, Howarth looked as though he hadn't been hassled by the police recently. Best not to get Whitfield all worked up. He was the sudden type who might go out there without enough information.

Bill Perkins might know something about Howarth. The contractor wasn't in his county, but Bill got around and heard things. Restless, Adam left Brad with instructions to call if any information came in, and drove to the Sheriff's home.

The house in Owen fronted on a short, curving street. A garden filled the front yard, daffodils and early tulips at this time of year, but overflowed with colorful flowers by July. Bill's wife was the gardener, Bill the muscle.

Bill met him at the door. "Come in, come in. What can I do for you?"

"I need your help again, Bill."

"How about coffee first?"

The two men walked back to the cheerful kitchen where Bill's wife poured coffee and left.

"What's this about?"

Adam recounted his visit to Howarth. Bill didn't know much about him, except that he employed some tough-looking men on his site whose only job seemed to be to stare at strangers and the workingmen. Bill knew guys who quit because of it, in spite of excellent wages.

"I think he is on the wrong side of the line, but I don't have anything to go on."

"That was my feeling too."

The two men chatted for a while, then Adam left. No word from Brad, but he didn't expect much on a Sunday.

Brad waved an Interpol warrant at him when he walked in the squad room.

"We've got him, Adam. Interpol wants him. It's just Jennifer and Davis' bad luck that they tried to blackmail a really bad guy."

Howarth, or Howaravich, a well-known crime figure in Moscow, fled the country when even he couldn't buy enough protection, or intimidate enough police to keep himself secure. He was wanted on an Interpol warrant for gunrunning activities and in Canada for drug and prostitution ring organizations.

Adam notified the FBI and also called Bill Perkins to let him know what was in the works. The FBI field agent in Burlington was coming to Culver's Mills to go over Adam's data. Bill said he hoped they wouldn't let the guy escape while they made sure of Adam's information.

The agent, Calvin Maunder, spent some time going over the evidence of blackmail they had accumulated even though it didn't really affect his case against the Russian. The bureau decided to move against Howarth in the morning when his wife drove the little boy to school. As far as they knew, there were three men besides Howarth in the house. Maunder was reluctant to let Adam and Bill take part in the assault, but caved in when they reminded him that local charges of murder were pending against the man.

Chapter Twenty-Six

O n Monday morning Anne was happily making plans to go home. She still wanted to have dinner with Adam and left a message after she had made a tentative reservation at Evan's. She was finishing her morning coffee, sitting in Catherine's kitchen, watching the raindrops coursing down the windowpanes when the phone rang.

"Anne, Thomas Beauchamp is on the line for you," Catherine called.

"Good morning, Anne."

"Good morning."

"Would you like to go to Burlington with me for lunch?"

"I'd love to, but I've just arranged to go to dinner with Adam Davidson. Would we be back in time?"

"Sure, we'll fly. You don't have any problem with small planes, I hope?"

"Oh, no. I love to fly."

"I'll pick you up around noon if that suits you."

"Perfect."

Anne hung up the phone smiling and told Catherine her plans.

Thomas' plane, a little two-seater painted a bright yellow, waited for them at the local airport. One landing strip, a ticket agent, and a drink machine served the commuter airline and a few private planes.

Thomas handed her into the passenger seat and buckled the belt for her. Thomas likes to look after women, she thought.

When they were halfway to Burlington, the rain stopped, and the drenched landscape below glowed bright green and gold in the sunshine.

Anne had only been in the city once before, on her honeymoon, although she didn't share that with Thomas.

The university town had several trendy restaurants, but thinking Anne would prefer a slightly more casual place, Thomas led her through an alley, into the stone-paved courtyard of an old stable and up to the second floor. The high-ceilinged room, flooded with sunshine, delighted Anne.

"What a lovely spot, Thomas."

"The kitchen is good too. The chefs were doing Asian fusion here long before it became fashionable. Now the chef is moving back to more traditional American, but lighter than is usual

"Again ahead of the curve, I think."

Thomas and Anne talked on and on, lingering until Thomas said, "You're going back to Canada soon, I imagine?"

"Yes, tomorrow."

"I'd like to see you again. Could we meet in Toronto?"

"I'd love to. I have a small condominium on the waterfront. My husband and I used it for city vacations."

"How long has it been since your husband died?"

"Two years."

"And how are you?"

"Much better. The first year was hard, but I think I'm okay now. The grief sits much further down nowadays, and I moved on with my life. I loved him very much, Thomas."

Anne's eyes searched Thomas's face.

"As I loved my wife, but you do have to start to live again. Are you going back to work?"

"I don't think so. At least, not what I was doing. I may do some locums. Filling in for vacationing pediatricians," she said in reply to his quizzical look.

"I found work was engrossing and distracting. That helped," Thomas said.

"I was too distracted for my work. My practice involved emotionally upset children and I had difficulty maintaining my own equilibrium."

"I understand. I'll be in Toronto next week. Perhaps we could meet?"

"I'll give you my numbers," Anne said as she pulled out a business card and scribbled on the back. "I think we should be going, Thomas. It's almost three."

Thomas kissed her at Catherine's door. The first kiss since Michael had died. Later, when telling Catherine about her day, she said she felt delighted about the kiss. "No guilt, either. I am so happy about that, Catherine. I really can get on with my life now."

Chapter Twenty-Seven

An overcast Monday morning threatened rain. Perfect, Adam thought, they'd be doing this in a downpour. He and Pete checked out rifles and rain gear and drove to Burlington to the FBI field office. It was about 7:00 am when they parked next to Bill Perkins' truck.

The field office was in a newer office building, with a marble lobby, and a few tall potted plants near the entrance, their soil dotted with butts from the smokers who huddled around the door. Large men in full assault gear and two or three in the black raincoats familiar from television and movies crowded the office on the fourth floor. They moved in beside Bill at the back of the crowd listening to Maunder review their approach to the Howarth residence.

Bill leaned past Pete to whisper to Adam.

"We're going to be at the back of the pack, fellows."

"That suits me fine, Bill," Adam said. "I don't think the defenses are as limited as Maunder does. Are they sure the kid and his mother will be out of the house?"

"Yeah, they aren't going to move until they see them arrive at the school. Someone is going to detain the mother, so he says."

Maunder called an end to the briefing and told the men to wait in their vehicles until they got a call that the mother left the house. He pushed through the crowd towards Adam, shook his hand, and asked if he wanted to ride with the first vehicle.

"Not at all, Calvin, I want to be able to have a word with him afterwards."

"Sure, no problem. "

He gave Adam a pitying glance. The agent was pumped and didn't understand anyone who didn't want to be in on the assault.

~

The unmarked vehicles moved slowly down the quiet residential street. There were still kids on bicycles on their way to school and a few early morning walkers. As they got closer to their target, the police warned people to go back into their homes. At 8:30 am, the radios crackled and an officer with a bullhorn addressed the house.

"This is the FBI with a warrant for Pavel Howarth. The house is surrounded. Come out with your hands behind your heads and lie face down on the ground."

The rain pelted down and distant thunder rumbled but otherwise, silence and no movement visible inside the house. The waiting officers shifted, repositioned their weapons, checked sight-lines, anticipating the order to attack but Maunder patient.

"No action," he said into the radio connecting all the men.

Again the bullhorn roared out the command to surrender; again nothing.

Adam wondered if they were too late or if something he did the day before alerted the Russian.

Shots hit the ground in front of Maunder and his bullhorn. At the same time, Adam could hear gunfire from the back of the house. Adam and Pete were partway down the block across the street. From where he stood Adam could see the back corner of the garage. A figure crept along the wall of the garage and disappeared into the hedge on the neighboring property. He yelled at Bill to tell Maunder someone was escaping to the east and at Pete to come with him and sprinted across the road.

He and Pete took opposite sides of the neighboring house. A woman appeared at the window, pointing into her backyard as she knocked at the glass to get his attention. Adam's hands motioned her down. A burst of gunfire and the splatter of bullets into the wall behind him told him his quarry saw her too. Shots came from the other side of the yard. Adam crept around a shrub that masked the corner of the building. The shooter's back was to him; his rifle aimed towards Pete.

"Hold it. Police."

The man spun around with a snarl, bringing his rifle up to shoot. Adam smashed his head with the stock of his gun. The shooter slumped to his knees and then to the ground, his wound pouring blood. Adam called for the paramedics.

"Is the bastard still alive, boss?"

"Yeah. Go check the house. He shot at a woman who was pointing him out to me."

"Silly bitch."

"Make sure she's okay."

Shots rang out behind him as he held the wound of the man on the ground. The Russian's chest moved, not much, but it moved. Adam got out of the way of the paramedics as they arrived, and ran across the road to Bill.

"We got the Russian, but I don't know if I killed him. I hit him pretty hard."

"Ruskis have hard heads. He'll live to face it."

Across the street, tear gas and the sounds of coughing from the people inside drifted from the windows of the house. The front door cracked open, and weapons came hurtling out. Two gagging men followed, doing their best to keep their hands behind their heads and their eyes clear enough to see. They fell to the ground, the agents cuffed them and pulled them to the waiting van. An ambulance drove away code four, with lights flashing and siren wailing.

Maunder strode across the road.

"Thought you only wanted to talk to him. I didn't know you wanted to club him to death," he said.

"Bastard was going to shoot Pete," Adam said. "Where the hell is he anyway? I sent him to check on the woman in the house."

As he spoke, Pete came out the front door and loped across the street.

"She was some scared, Adam. Her kitchen is a mess. Bullet holes every-where. Did you get everybody?" he said to Maunder.

"Yeah, we did. Are you coming back to the office?" he asked Adam.

"No, We'll go back to Culver's Mills. I'll email you a report."

With that, Bill, Pete and Adam left. It was only 9:05am. It felt like tomorrow.

When they left Bill in Greenbank, he said, "Good job, but you took a big chance going into the guy's place by yourself the first time. Your man Brad couldn't have helped you if Howarth decided to kill you."

"I told him I was collecting for the Boys and Girls Club. He gave me a promise to donate 1,000 dollars."

"A thousand! I wonder if you can collect?" The sheriff drove off, chuckling.

~

Adam spent some time writing a report to send to Maunder. He covered the part he and Pete played in the morning's drama. He listened for the call he knew would come. In spite of Howarth's head injury, Maunder hoped to question him, and if not him, at least the two captured with him and the wife. The answers would go a long way, he hoped, in winding up his unsolved cases.

When Maunder called, he told Adam he could place Howarth at the scene of both Davis's murder and Lauder's, but not at Jennifer's. He still couldn't talk to Howarth, but the two thugs rolled over on him. The gun he carried had killed both men.

Adam thanked him and said he would call Bill. That left him with Jennifer. It was hard to believe two murderers were operating in their little town. On the other hand, if Howarth were a shooter, why would he crush her skull instead? The crime seemed unpremeditated, especially if the murder weapon was the carpet ball she had on her desk. He called Maunder back.

"Calvin, is there any way we can interview that guy soon?"

"I just got off the phone with his lawyer. The bastard is claiming diplomatic immunity."

"What? I thought he was wanted in Russia too."

"That was before the change in government. The secret police are in power over there with Putin as president or whatever he is now. I figure Howarth was one of them. A lot of them turned to crime with glasnost. I think they're taking care of their own."

"Where does that leave us?"

"The lawyer said he would let his client talk to us, but he couldn't be charged with any crime. So we'll have to deport him."

"I want to talk to him about Jennifer Smith's murder."

"His alibi is good for that one. The lawyer said he was in a meeting with him and the executive council of the planning board that didn't break up until 2:00 am."

"Did it check out?"

"Yeah, it did."

"Thanks for doing that, Calvin. Talk to you later."

"No problem."

After he hung up, Adam sat with his head in his hands for a few long minutes before he called Bill Perkins to give him the news. Bill reminded him there were still blackmailing leads other than to Howarth to follow up and that a woman like Jennifer could have aroused homicidal feelings in a lot of people. And, Adam remembered, there was still the damn carpet ball. Where was it?

Chapter Twenty-Eight

A dam was back in Burlington the next morning. Howarth waited for deportation, and Maunder brought him to the Bureau building for interviews. Adam took coffee in with him.

Howarth recognized Adam when the guard brought him into the windowless interview room.

"You, I should have known."

His head was still bandaged where Adam had clubbed him.

"Look, Howarth, you're out from under on these murders because of the immunity thing, so it won't hurt you to give me a little information."

Adam passed a pack of cigarettes and a container of coffee to him.

"What's in it for me?"

Howarth squinted at him across the table.

"What could I do for you?"

"I need to make sure the woman and the kid are okay. She didn't have anything to do with my business. She's a good mother. She should keep the kid."

He stared across at Adam, his eyes red-rimmed. Adam heard that Russians were sentimental, but he hadn't expected this. He thought for a moment.

"I'll check up on them for you and try to make sure she keeps the boy. You didn't marry her?"

"No, I got a wife in Russia, but this one, she is special to me."

"So she won't be going to meet you."

"No."

"I'll see them tomorrow and call you."

"Good. Good. What do you want to know?"

The Russian relaxed as he sat back in his chair.

"First, did you kill Jennifer Smith?"

"That bitch. No, I didn't kill her. I am happy someone did. One hundred thousand dollars that pair took from me."

Adam wondered why such a violent guy didn't kill her long ago.

"Why did you pay?"

"She and that snake Davis said that they had information that would be mailed to the feds if one of them died, some kind of immigration record. After she died, I sent Lauder and another guy to look for it. They found nothing. Nothing. Davis called—more money, or he would make sure they knew where I was. He thought I killed her too. So I killed the creep. I figured —why leave a loose end—and saw Lauder. He was in a panic. You know the rest."

"How did you hear that she was dead?"

"Davis called me."

"What about the third guy?"

"Gone."

"Was she blackmailing any other wiseguys that you heard of?"

"No."

Howarth stretched, yawned, and lit one of the cigarettes.

"She was a mean, nasty bitch," he went on. "She boasted everyone from rich men to poor grandmothers were on her list and they all paid. Is that all?"

"That's all."

Adam knocked on the door for the guard and Howarth strutted away, down the corridor. The desk clerk told Adam they released the woman to go home. No one knew what happened to the kid. Child protection, they thought.

The suburban neighborhood where Howarth lived looked back to normal, except for the yellow tape, tattered and snapping in the wind. The few onlookers stared as he turned into the driveway. Pockmarks from bullet holes dotted the front of the house and plastic covered the windows. Maybe Howarth's construction crews could get over here and fix them before the company wound down, he thought.

The doorbell ringing brought the small blonde woman. This time she spoke to him through the crack in the door.

"What do you want?"

"I'm Lieutenant Davidson, Mrs. Howarth. I came last week. Do you remember?"

"Yes, I remember. Paul called and told me I should talk to you."

"May I come in?"

She opened the door and let him into the front foyer. The gun battle and the teargas grenades made quite a mess. The little boy sat the top of the stairs. His mother saw him too.

"Go to your room, Paulie."

"Then you didn't have any trouble getting him back? Paul wanted me to check."

"No. They want to supervise for a while. I don't care. I'm not going anywhere."

"Will you be okay for money to live and repair the house?"

"I'm selling the house as soon as I can. It belongs to me, and it's all paid for. As long as the government doesn't try to take it from me, there'll be enough for us to live on if I'm careful."

"What's your name?"

"Karen."

"You don't want to go to Russia?"

They sat in the huge over-decorated room where he had talked to Howarth. She turned her head away as her eyes filled with tears.

"I can't go there. He has a wife there, and I want little Paul to grow up here where he belongs. He is an American child. His father wants him to be an American child, too."

"Is there anything I can do for you?"

"No, just tell Paul that we are okay."

"I'll do that."

Adam shook her hand, but she didn't get up, and he left her with her face in her hands and her shoulders shaking. He let himself out.

On the way back to Culver's Mills, he called the jail to speak to Howarth. Adam reassured him that Karen and his son were well and going to be together. He got mumbled thanks and a few words in Russian as a reply.

When Adam got back to the office, he found a message on his desk that Anne called to say goodbye, and that she planned to leave Wednesday morning and did he want to have dinner with her before she went. What he wanted was for her to stay. It was 5:00pm, so he signed out and headed home to change.

Anne made tentative reservations at Evan's. He arranged to pick her up at 7:00pm, fed Sam and called Erin. If he wasn't too late, he wanted to tell her about the arrest before she heard details around town or on the news.

When Anne and Adam walked into the restaurant, he showed her the carpet balls in the large bowl in the foyer. He took a minute to look at each one, but none of them had the pattern that Erin had described. They sat at a table in one of the slight alcoves formed by the bow windows at the front of the house.

"Would you like a Bloody Caesar, Anne?"

"Yes, thanks. But where did you learn to drink Bloody Caesars?"

"On a case in Montreal. We're close enough to the border and get enough Canadian tourists that all the bars here carry the ingredients and Canadian rye whisky."

"Were you there when the FBI arrested Howarth?"

"Yes."

He described the scene at the Howarth home to her as they waited for their drinks.

"I gave him a good hit for you, Anne."

"I can't say I'm sorry. He gave me some very bad moments."

"Do you have to go back tomorrow?"

"I've no reason to stay. I've finished all my research and found Margaret. Why do you ask?"

"I still need your help. The Russian killed Davis and Lauder and made the attacks on you, but there is no way he killed Jennifer. He has no reason to admit to the others and stonewall on this one. So I am short one killer and need to look at the other blackmail victims. Can you stay at least one more day and help Brad? The department could pay to put you up at Catherine's or any other place you wanted."

"I can stay, and won't say no to the bills being paid, but we've gone over most of those files, and Pete eliminated almost all of them by distance, where they were the night of the murder and so on."

"The only clues I have left are ones I can't find. The carpet ball, a house-keeper of the Culvers I haven't been able to talk to yet, and some anonymous victim in those files. Please stay."

"How can I say no? Will you let me have dinner now?"

After dinner, Adam drove Anne home and called on Erin on the way back. The lights in the shop were brighter at the back where she hunched over her computer.

"Come in. Did you have a nice dinner?"

"Excellent."

By now he was curious every time he came into the shop to see what the furniture arrangement was. Tonight's looked like the deck of a ship in the 1930's, with two deck chairs in fine old wood with worn plaid blankets adding a touch of color. The light of a tall lamp directed upwards reflected off the tin ceiling.

"What is that lamp called?"

"That's a torchiere. The chairs are from the Queen Elizabeth. I'm going to call the couple from Toronto about them. They told me they have a cottage at some place called Stoney Lake. From what they described these would be perfect for them."

"Very comfortable," commented Adam as he settled into one of them.

"Coffee?" Erin asked.

"Yes, thanks."

Adam described the scene at Howarth's arrest. He didn't want to frighten her, but he wanted her to know what his life was like. Concern and horror grew on her face as he told her about clubbing Howarth.

She shuddered.

"At least you didn't have to kill him. Is Pete okay?"

"Yes, he's fine. Pete takes this all in a day's work. I didn't want you to hear this on the news."

"You think that your work frightens me and horrifies me. It does frighten me. Of course, it does. Even in this small town, any day could bring life-threatening danger to you. But I am horrified, not by your work but at the— is evil too strong a word—that is all around you. I am appalled that Jennifer was an acquaintance, someone I saw almost every day, and never suspected she brought so much anguish into the lives of so many others. What did that man say, even a grandmother? How could she be so horrible?"

Adam reached across and took her hand. "I'm glad that bothers you and not my work in trying to stop it."

"Oh, no."

After a few more minutes of conversation, Adam got up to leave.

"By the way, Erin, you know the housekeeper at the Culvers, I think you said?"

"Just a little."

"What's her first name?"

"Beatrice."

Beatrice, he thought as he drove home. Where was Beatrice?

Chapter Twenty-Nine

Rain again. Adam pulled on his gear to go running at 6am. He wanted to be at work early to finish his report for Captain Naismith and to set Brad working on the files. Not a happy thought. Brad and Pete would assume the case was done.

But what Mrs. Ames wanted to tell him? When he got to the office, he would call and make an appointment with her.

He finished up his run and arrived at the office at 7:30. Brad came in at 8:00am

"Morning, Lieutenant."

"Morning. Come in and sit down."

Adam went over the events of Monday with him, including the news that they were short one murderer.

"Damn it. Is Maunder sure that the Russian's alibi is solid for the time of the murder?"

"Absolutely sure. He was tied up with a bunch of local politicians 'til way past the time she died. He has diplomatic immunity, too."

"What the fuck."

Brad knew that Adam didn't like swearing on the job, but this was more than Brad could believe.

"So the Russian Embassy says. Maunder did his best, but the guy's on a plane for Moscow this morning. He confessed to Davis and Lauder."

"Now what?"

"Back to the files. I asked Anne to come in and help again. She planned to go home, but she agreed to stay. I want you to check again in case we missed someone who could have been in town the night of the murder. Find Morrison and call the hospital about the wife."

As he finished giving Brad instructions Anne arrived, under her own steam this time, feeling a little safer with Howarth behind bars, she said.

After the morning ritual of coffee and small talk, he asked her to look for information on Beatrice Ames.

Mrs. Ames didn't answer the door at the Culver home. Adam sent the maid in search of Mrs. Culver or David Culver. He expected they might still be at breakfast and the maid showed him to the dining room. Naomi Culver sat at an oval dining table with a coffee pot and cups in front of her. Her son sat to her right.

"Do sit down, Mr. Davidson. Would you like some coffee?"

Apparently, she decided to be the gracious lady today. The last time he'd been here, she couldn't wait to see his back.

"Yes, thanks."

"I understand that you have the man in custody who committed these awful crimes."

That explained it. She thought the pressure was off her and her family.

"Yes, we arrested the man who killed the lawyer Stan Davis, and another man called Dave Lauder, but we don't think he killed Jennifer."

"Why on earth not?"

"I'm not at liberty to say, ma'am. I came here today to talk to Mrs. Ames. She left a message last week that she wanted to talk to me."

"Mrs. Ames is not here. She's on holiday for a week. I don't know where. Do you, David?" she asked.

"No," he said. "I don't discuss the housekeeper's personal plans with her. Why does she want to talk to you?"

"Perhaps she has information she thinks will help."

"You mean you're back to me as a suspect."

The china on the table jumped as his fist came down. "I did not kill that woman!'

"So you said, and we accepted it," Adam said. "I don't have any reason to think that she wants to talk about you. Mrs. Ames did have a private life outside this house. Would you have any idea where her mother lives?"

"None. We have an employment record. It might give an address. We also have references from where Mrs. Ames worked last. She worked here for about eight months."

"Could I have it and check her room? By the way, who drove her to town when she left? Did she say where she was going?"

Mrs. Culver answered, "She drove herself in her own car. I suppose we can let you look at her room, but we couldn't let you take anything."

"What kind of car?"

"An old Ford Taurus, grey," David said.

Adam stood up, and David led him towards the back of the house.

"She always locks her door," he said. "We insist on it so that there are no accusations of thefts."

The door, however, was not locked. Mrs. Ames's two small rooms, a sitting room and a bedroom, were empty of personal belongings, including the closets.

"I think you are going to need a new housekeeper," Adam said. "Did anyone see her leave?"

"We'll ask. All she told mother was that she was going to take a short vacation. Mother doesn't ask any questions because she thinks the staff are entitled to a private life."

Mrs. Culver found the employment record and the references. She called the maid, the gardener/chauffeur and the cook. No one saw Mrs. Ames leave and they weren't friendly.

"She was always going to the library on her day off," the maid said.

Adam thanked the Culvers and left. From his car, he tried to call Brad, but he was still out checking on the Morrisons.

Patient Inquiry at the hospital told Brad that Mrs. Morrison remained in the Intensive Care Unit. She lay in the first bed of the six-bed unit. Her chest rose and fell slowly in synchrony with the soft sounds of the ventilator. No chance of any interview today. The nurse at the desk said that her husband called but that he hadn't come in.

"Did you tell him we were involved?"

"Yes. Weren't we supposed to? All I said was that the police found her."

"Next time, don't volunteer."

"You might have mentioned that you didn't want anything told to the family. We don't keep anything from them, and he did ask."

"Ask what?"

"Who found her."

Brad called in and left a message for Adam that he was going out to talk to Morrison's brother.

The ancient glass in the door of the store was so bubbled and wavy that Brad couldn't really see in. Maybe Morrison couldn't see out, he thought.

The bell over the door tinkled as he went through. No customers, no canned music and no lights even though the store was open. Brad called out.

"Ted, it's Brad Compton, Culver's Mills Police. I need to talk to you."

Silence. Goods packed the store: racks of clothes, shelves full of garden gnomes and such, a few books, and hats with the name of the village on them. There were only two ways out, and one of them was behind Brad. Past the racks and close to the change rooms, a door opened to the rear. Brad walked through towards the back door.

"No," someone shouted.

Pain exploded in Brad's head.

On the way back from his interview with the Culvers, Adam stopped for take-out at the Tim Horton's, remembering that Anne liked French vanilla cappuccino. He got regular for himself, and a pack of Tim Bits. Tim Horton's was his favorite Canadian export, that and Bloody Caesars.

The information at the office was good and bad. They found Mrs. Ames' social security records, but the address was a box number in Burlington. Anne, however, found a B.A. listed in Jennifer's files. the initials IN followed. Jennifer wrote a ship's name next to the listing, but Anne hadn't found it yet.

Adam paced between his office and the squad room- waiting. The phone rang.

"Lieutenant Davidson, this is the ambulance service. An officer's down, in Pine Grove. Meet the ambulance at the emergency room, please."

Only Brad was out. Pine Grove meant the Morrisons. They'd no reason to think that the brother was involved in any of this. Why had he let him go without backup? Adam beat himself up with remorse the rest of the way to the hospital. He parked beside the ambulance bay and heard the stomach-knotting sounds of the ambulance siren as he ran towards the bay door. As they swung open the doors to the ambulance box he hung on the door with relief as Brad grinned at him from the stretcher, pale but alive and alert.

"I'm okay, boss. I was only out for a few minutes. I could hear the 911 operator calling from the phone. She said the call came through about five minutes before I woke up."

"Who was there?"

"I don't know. No one was there when I came to."

The door closed behind the stretcher.

Adam waited in the corridor that separated the nursing station from the trauma room. When they were busy, you couldn't find a nurse. They would be spread out in the department's different areas. Three separate groups stood talking. Two doctors mumbled into telephones, dictating he thought. A tall redheaded nurse caught his eye and walked over to him.

"Hi, Adam. Is it one of your men that the guys brought in?"

Adam had known Cassidy Waite for all the years he worked in the Culver's police. She arrived in town, a single mom, with two kids, the year he started. She worked her way up from casual shifts at the hospital to be in charge most days in the emergency room. Adam knew her in the way police know the emergency room nurses: Saturday nights bringing in drunks and the overdosed, gunshot wounds or a sometimes a tragic motor vehicle accident or drowning. Cassidy was steady, and Adam was always happy when she was on duty.

"Yes, Brad Compton. You know him?"

"Sure. Big guy, young with a broken nose. Right?"

"That's him. Can you find out if he's okay? I need to talk to him."

She was back in a few minutes, assuring him the Brad was fine. They sent him for a CAT scan to be sure, but the doctor didn't think there was any real problem. He could go with him to the procedure if he wanted.

The CAT scan was in the basement of the hospital, an add-on after the original construction. Because it was underground, the staff hung paintings on the wall of landscapes and flowers and decorated the desk and corners with artificial flowers. Three chairs and Adam filled the tiny waiting room. The nurse wheeled Brad's stretcher expertly into the CAT scan room.

While the technician prepared Brad for the scan, Adam got the story of his trip to Pine Grove again.

"So any idea who hit you?" he asked when Brad got to the part about the pain in his head.

"None. When I woke up, I could hear the 911 operator yelling down the phone. I guess whoever called her left the line open. She said it was only five minutes from the call 'til I was talking to her. Ouch."

"Sorry, Brad. I didn't want to interrupt your story," she said as she hung the bag of IV fluid. "Now I'm going to inject some contrast. You've never had a reaction during as x-ray, have you?"

"No."

"This one gives you a very warm sensation that starts at your head and goes to your toes and is gone. It doesn't hurt, but some people feel it as hotter than other people do," she explained as she wheeled him over and into the machine.

Brad's head slid in to the opening, held in place by some small sandbags.

"Whoa, that is warm."

"Relax."

"I'll try," Brad said, preparing to daydream a little.

"Okay, we're done."

"Already? When can I go?"

"Take it easy, Brad. The doctor wants to check the images before you can leave."

Twenty minutes later Adam was back in the office, leaving Brad at his mother's home to sleep off his headache.

Anne couldn't go any further without Brad to help her, so Adam suggested she go back to Catherine's. It was well past time for lunch.

The Morrison brothers occupied his mind. He remembered that they grew up over in Pine Grove with a father who was been a small-time contractor and handyman. The older one went to the local high school a few years ahead of Adam, but he hadn't been around for years after that. Ted, the younger one, took over the small store that his mother kept. It had been the beer and chips store for kids spending a night at the lake when Adam was young. From Brad's description, it carried a bit more now but hadn't changed much otherwise.

Adam poured himself a coffee and put his feet up on his desk. He hadn't heard of any scams involving Jake Morrison, or Ted. Joe Brearley, a local real estate agent of the old style, mostly working out of the front seat of his car, and at the local diner. He rented a nominal office in a tiny strip mall. Chances of finding him there were nil, Adam thought. He called to Angie, the clerk who tried to keep the paperwork on track, for the phone number of the agent's office. The machine was on when he called. Maybe the diner.

Peg worked at the till, doing bills or receipts or something when he came in about 3:00pm, a downtime until the school kids arrived after 4:00pm.

"Hey, Adam. What brings you here this time of day?"

"I'm looking for Joe Brearley. Does he have a regular time in here?"

Peg laughed. "Does he ever. Twice. Before he heads off to the office to pick up the paperwork for whatever deals he had going about 8:45am. Has a coffee, reads the paper and takes a cup for the road. I don't know where he eats lunch. Next time I see him is about 3:10pm if he doesn't have a client to ferry around.

"So any time now?" Adam asked.

"With any luck."

"Then I'll have a piece of your apple pie and a glass of milk."

Adam finished his pie and swallowed the last of his milk when the door opened, and Joe came in with a cheerful greeting for Peg and a nod to Adam. Brearley was a compact man, short and square, with thinning blond hair and odd colored eyes, one blue, one brown. A large head on the small body gave him a gnomish look. When he settled at a table with his coffee, Adam went over.

"Could I have a word with you, Joe. Adam Davidson, Culver's police," he said as he sat down.

"Sure, why not?"

Both the eyes looked anxious, but Adam was used to that.

"I'm looking for Jake Morrison. Have you seen him lately or done any business with him?"

"Jake? Sure. What's he done?"

The laugh was nervous too.

"Nothing as far as I know. His wife is ill, and I need to locate him. Have you been in contact today? I know you get around quite a bit."

Adam leaned back and took a sip of coffee.

"Yeah, sure I do. But I didn't see Jake today. I'm listing those houses he is building out on the lake, but I haven't talked to him for a few days. Did you try his office?"

"I thought he worked on site?"

"He has an office above mine, in the back. I didn't see his truck this morning, and I haven't been back."

"How is he to do business with?"

"He's okay. He's working on a shoestring, but the bills get paid."

"When did he come back here, do you know?"

"I don't really know anything about him, Lieutenant. What's that got to do with finding him? He has a brother. Why don't you ask him?"

"Any reason you don't want to answer the question?"

"No, no. I don't want to get him pissed off. I have to do business with the guy."

"So when did he come back?"

"Couple, three years ago. Brought that Viet woman with him."

"He wasn't old enough to go to Nam, was he?"

"Sure. Just at the end. He come out on the helicopters."

"With the woman?"

"Don't know anything about her."

"Do you know the brother?"

Joe settled back in his chair, relaxed. Getting used to him? Or was he moving away from a sensitive spot, as the conversation turned to Ted?

"Oh, yeah. He runs that store in Pine Grove since his mother died. Nice guy. Jake always led him around by the nose when they were young. Now, I don't know. What's up, Davidson?" he went on suspiciously. "What's this got to do with finding a guy whose wife is sick?"

"I need to talk to Jake, Joe, and I can't say more."

"Neither can I. I gotta go."

Suddenly he was up and gone, leaving a five dollar bill on the table for Peg.

Adam ambled to the window and watched Brearley's car disappear in the direction of his office.

The clock in the tower on the courthouse struck four, a deep note playing against the church bells from the other end of the square. Adam drove out to the strip mall.

The mall was hardly worthy of the name: a gas station at one end, not a chain, but one of those that sell cut-rate and poor quality gasoline; a convenience store attached to that; a liquor store; and Joe's office at the end.

Brearley looked up as Adam came in, not happy to see him.

"Again. Didn't we talk long enough? I've got work to do."

Blustering and scared. What the hell did he have to be afraid of?

"Sure. But I want to check Morrison's office," Adam said.

"Don't you need a warrant or something?"

"I don't want to search the place. I want to see if he's there."

"So what are you bothering me for?"

"Aren't you the landlord?"

"Yes, but I can't let you in."

"Come on, Joe. Stop dicking around."

Adam yanked open the door.

"Let's go."

"Okay, okay. It's around the back."

Upkeep wasn't Joe's strong suit as a landlord. The paint at the back had seen better days, and the railing on the stairs was more hazard than help. Joe was puffing at the top and fumbled with the key after Adam pounded on the door. Adam pulled him back as he attempted to go in first.

"In case, okay, Joe?"

No Jake. No furniture. A phone sat abandoned in the middle of the floor.

"What the fuck."

Joe's face turned red to his ears.

"Looks like your tenant's taken French leave," Adam said.

"What?"

"Gone. Vamoosed. Did he owe you money?"

"No. In fact, I owed him. Why would he do this? What's going on, Lieutenant?"

"So far he's been a guy with a sick wife. But now I want to talk to him. If he calls you or you see him, call me. Understand?"

"Sure, sure I will."

Adam left the salesman shaking and pouring himself a drink in the office.

Thinking that the woman might have come out of her coma, Adam drove back to the hospital. The intensive care unit was on the third floor opposite a nursing station. He buzzed for entry and walked down the short hall, passed the curtained patient cubicles to the desk.

Alison Blalock, the head nurse, looked up from the paperwork that is the time-consuming bane of every nurse's existence. She knew Adam from their work with the local Boys and Girls Club.

"Hi, Adam. How are you?"

"Fine, thanks. Is Mrs. Morrison awake?"

"Sure. She woke up this morning, and we discharged her about two o'clock."

"What? Where was my guard?"

"He had to leave. Big MVA on the four-lane. We're getting two. We put her in a taxi when she insisted on leaving. I don't know where she went. She wouldn't give a destination until we left. Sorry, Adam."

Adam thanked her and waited to explode until he reached his car.

He called Pete to meet him at the lake. He wanted back up. These people seemed to be desperate and desperate people did dangerous and stupid things. On the way, he put out a bulletin on the Morrison vehicle. They probably changed cars if they were running from them.

≈

Pete waited for him at the rock-cut. Adam told him they would take his truck as he went around to get the shotgun out of the trunk.

"Who are we after, Adam?"

"The Morrisons."

"You're kidding. I didn't figure them for real bad guys."

"I think they were the ones who hit Brad. One of them anyway. The other one called 911. At least that's how I figure it."

After Adam brought Pete up to speed on the Morrisons, they drove the rest of the long lane in silence. It was dark now. The trees bending overhead kept the light from the setting sun off the road. Pete cut the headlights before they rounded the curve to the house. No lights in the windows. The silver-tinged, purple lake, the brightest spot in the landscape, lay still beyond the house. They saw no movement as they walked up the gravel path to the house. The path stopped at three steps up to the deck and the front door. Clear cedar for the deck and the door. No expense spared here. Like all lake houses, most of the windows were on the waterside. The high small windows to one side were likely in the bedrooms, he thought, trying to remember the layout. No answer to their knocks.

Adam waved Pete around to the front on one side while he took the other. No movement inside. Pete reached the front and called him.

"Adam! Doors are wide open. I'm going to check the boathouse."

Adam watched Pete's loping run then turned back to the house. He groped for a light switch. The pot lights in the ceiling glowed remotely. Nothing much changed since he carried Morrison's wife out. He waited for Pete.

Something heavy hit the water, the sound echoing off the building. Splashing and Pete's voice calling. An engine roared.

Christ, I hope Pete's not under that propeller he thought as he ran to the waterfront.

The sound of the powerful boat distanced. Pete's head bobbed in the wake.

"Pete," he yelled. "You okay?"

"Yeah. That son of a bitch. Throw me a line. My gear's weighing me down."

A ring hung on the boathouse. Under-water steps led up to the wall along the shore. Adam threw the ring and pulled Pete in to the stairs.

"What happened?"

"When I got to the boathouse, I found all the doors locked," said Pete as pulled off his boots and wrung the water out of his socks. "I walked down beside it to see if the waterside door was open. Look at this," he interrupted himself as he poured water from his holster, "damn things aren't waterproof. As I turned the corner, he came at me and shoved me in. She or someone was in the boat because he shouted—go, go—and the engine turned over. I swam hard as I could toward the shore. That bastard didn't care where I was. He just missed me as he came out of the slip."

"Which way?"

"Up the lake. He's long gone. He'll have a car at the marina at the head of the lake. It's closed at this time of night so the guys will be gone. He'll drive away."

"Someone will have seen the vehicle."

"Maybe. But he's a good customer. They may not have "noticed"." By now Pete had his shirt off and was wringing fouled lake water, scented with gasoline and fish, out of it.

"Do you think we can requisition some towels for me from the house, Adam, since he's the one who put me in the lake?"

"Damn right."

Pete muttered colorful descriptions of Morrison's probable antecedents and current practices as they walked back to the house. He was shaking in the cold air.

"Take off the rest of your stuff, Pete. I'll find you a towel and some clothes." Adam said as he flicked on lights on his way into the bedroom.

Closets and drawers stood open, but still full. They didn't much, he thought. One drawer yielded a grey sweat suit and socks. He grabbed towels from a shelf in the bathroom. Pete lay on the white sofa, shivering and now sleepy.

"Wake up, Pete,' Adam shook him roughly. "You dry off and put these clothes on. You're hypothermic. That water can't be more than fifty degrees, since it's been so damn cold."

"Sleepy." Pete's voice was thick.

"I know." Adam pulled the shirt over Pete's head. "Put these pants on. I'm going to find some tea or bourbon or something."

There was tea. He made it strong with several spoons of sugar, a remedy his mother used for cold and shock. Adam wrapped Pete in a blanket and forced half a mug of tea down. Pete stopped shivering and managed his lop-sided grin.

"You going to leave a note for Morrison, Adam. Explain why we stole his clothes and drank his tea?"

"No. I'll apologize right after I arrest him for assault."

"Do you make him for the murderer?"

"Maybe. He was being blackmailed. At least he was on Jennifer's list. You okay to go back to town?"

"I think so."

Adam dropped Pete off at home with instructions for hot drink and sleep. He was going back to the office and to see Erin. He'd leave Morrison to the county boys for now.

Chapter Thirty

The next morning Anne began to feel the stirrings of an old familiar need. Too much time cooped up in an office. She needed to get out and about. Maybe she and Catherine could safely go to lunch, now the Russian was out of the picture.

"Sure," Catherine said. "We can go out past Pine Grove. Ariel Dawson runs a small tearoom in her house. It is beautifully restored, and her husband is an excellent chef. There is an antique store on the property and another over the stone bridge. The bridge is lovely."

"Will it be open?"

"I'll phone."

The stone bridge reminded Anne of one in a village near her hometown. The one she remembered had five arches, this one only three, but with the same grace and beauty. The spring floodwaters under the bridge hid the treacherous rapids Catherine had described to her on the way. A charming building of the same stone, housing an antique store, faced the bridge on the other side of the river. They decided to return after lunch.

A long curve up a hill and a right turn into a steep lane took them to the Bed and Breakfast (and lunch) owned by Ariel, Catherine's friend.

The view from a bench overlooking the valley was English watercolor perfect. Downriver and a hundred feet below, flat sheets of rock jutted into the rapids. Small islands of drowned trees marked the flood line. A canopy of forest on either side framed the view. A solitary red figure cast a fishing line from the near shore.

Catherine called her, and she turned to walk up to the cottage with her.

Green-framed French doors opened off the porch that wrapped around the house, and into the low-ceilinged dining room. The day was warm enough to sit outside, and so they did.

The high screened windows looked out over the expanse of the river to the hills beyond. Anne and Catherine chattered on about their mutual interests in gardening and reading and a little about Anne's work for Adam. As served their desserts, Anne noted another couple had come in at some point. Odd, Anne thought. They look like Adam's description of the Morrisons, a big blonde man and a tiny oriental woman, except she was in the hospital as far as Anne knew. Adam wanted to talk to him.

"Catherine, do you recognize the couple by the window?"

"No, I don't think I've ever seen them before."

"Do you think you could ask Ariel without letting them notice?"

"Sure, I'll try."

It didn't work. At least Anne didn't think so. Catherine trailed around the room, asking Ariel about the paintings and asking about the other couple very quietly, but somehow the man suspected. Anne thought he noticed Catherine's faint nod.

"Let's go on to the antique store," Catherine suggested.

The parking area for the store overlooked the river as it ran under the bridge. The town had built a cedar-planked lookout, over the water, but with the river so high it was fenced off.

Small rooms, one with a few pieces of antique furniture, dishes and collectibles, another with reproduction kitchenware, large white bowls, splatter-ware pie pans and the like, and a third with local crafts, crammed the small stone building. The door opened as Anne came down the stairs from the second floor. Morrison's large frame filled the doorway. He moved aside to let them pass and then followed them outside.

A grey truck, a Chev maybe, stood close to Catherine's van. Morrison's wife sat on the passenger side. As they crossed the road, a car came around the bend off the bridge, cutting Morrison off from them for a moment before it pulled into the parking lot beside Anne's car.

"Catherine, run to the car, lock yourself in and call 911. I'm afraid of what he might do."

"But, Anne—"

"Go."

Anne raced to a narrow path that led under the bridge. Morrison bellowed behind her. She stumbled down the steep, slippery path, onto one of the broad sheets of rock that marked the shoreline. Anne played in places like this as a child. She scrabbled across the granite, using her hands for balance, to a narrow ledge under the first arch. As she edged along, she heard Morrison cursing and telling her he wanted to talk to her.

The river lapped at the ledge, but Anne knew it was swift and deep in spite of its placid surface. What had she done? There was no way off at the other end.

"Hey," Morrison yelled at her as he leaned around the arch in front of her.

Anne lost her grip on the stones and clutched at the wall as her legs were caught by the strong current. Her fingers, scraping against the stones, caught on something. An iron ring. Anne held on as the river tore at her legs. She kept her head above the water, enough to breathe. In the distance, Catherine shrieked her name, but she couldn't answer. It took all she had to fight the current and keep her grasp on the ring. It won't be long, she thought. She'd have to let go soon. Her hands were numbed. Maybe she should let herself go and slip under the water. Maybe she could swim out of this. Maybe the rapids are covered deep enough.

Catherine called Adam from the car and watched unbelieving, as Anne ran under the bridge. The river was treacherous and there was no way off. Anne's hands held onto a ring drilled into the rock above the water line.

The car that cut Morrison off belonged to Ted Atkins. He bolted down the path to where Catherine stood, horror-stricken.

"There's a boat up the river. Come on. It will take two of us."

Catherine clutched his arm.

"Morrison's still out here. He might kill her."

"We can't stop him if he's going to, but she will drown if we don't get her out of the river."

Atkins pulled Catherine along the river and into the boat. She found a life-ring in the boat as he struggled with the motor. The engine caught, and they were in midstream. On land, Morrison ran back to his truck. It disappeared across the bridge.

Then they were under the arch where Anne struggled to keep her head above the water.

"Hurry, Ted, hurry," Catherine said.

Anne clung to the ring. She concentrated on her hands, willing them not to let go. An engine roared above the deep rumble of the rapids. The sound came closer. Her legs, would he stay away from her legs? The engine died.

"Anne, I'm putting a ring over your head. Try to put your arms through one at a time."

The ring fell against her arms.

"I can't. I'll not be able to hold on with one hand."

"Just for a second. Then you can hold the preserver. It's the only way."

Was that Adam's voice? How did he get here so fast? Taking a breath, Anne let go with one hand, clawed at the canvas, and held on. For dear life. Now she knew what that meant.

"Now your other hand. Do it, Anne," the voice that couldn't be Adam, commanded.

The iron ring was solid, attached. What if she lost it? Was she going to stay in the water forever? She let go and grasped the life preserver.

But now the river took her, pulling her downstream.

"Adam."

Did she scream? She didn't have energy left to scream.

"We have you."

The line tightened, and arms lifted her, knocking her ribs against the gunnel.

"Thank you," she whispered.

She grabbed Catherine's hand. At the dock, the paramedics wrapped her in blankets and gave her something hot to drink.

"Morrison, did you get him?" she asked Adam who appeared beside her when she could speak again.

"No."

"I'm sorry. I was so afraid he was going to kill us."

Abruptly, she sobbed, turning her face into Catherine's shoulder.

Adam waited until the ambulance left and asked Ted, "Which way did he turn at the bridge?"

"Left."

Left, away from Pine Grove, where his brother lived, and away from Culver's Mills. No border crossing.

"What's up that way?"

"Not much. Antara Lodge, a golf course and a few cottages, that's about it."

"Thanks a lot."

As Adam reached his car, he heard Ted shout, "Airport. There's a small landing strip."

Airport. Dust trailed behind him as he tore down the country road. He was almost past the sign before he saw it. A gravel track to the right ended a Quonset-hut hanger. Past the end of the runway, a small red plane disappeared to the north.

A thin grizzled man, dressed in coveralls, walked towards Adam, a folded paper in his hand.

"You Davidson?"

"Yeah"

"This is for you."

Davidson," he read, *I didn't kill that woman. Check with Stanbury Council. I was at their pig roast that night. I got personal reasons for leaving. Morrison.*

Personal reasons. What the hell were personal reasons?

"Do you know him?" he asked the mechanic.

"Just from here. Nothing else."

"Was he alone?"

"No, the wife was with him."

Maybe the brother could fill in the gaps.

Ted Morrison, when Adam found him, said his brother had lived in Canada for many years, with his Vietnamese wife. Denise had no papers for the United States, and he was afraid the Immigration service would find out about her if he had to answer questions. Denise was fragile, anxious and afraid. All she wanted to do was go back to Canada.

"She's all he has, Davidson. He'd do anything for her. He didn't kill the blackmailing bitch, though. He was at the pig roast till after midnight. Ask Ken Williams. He'll tell you. I was there too, so was Denise. I'm sorry about the officer he hit. I tried to stop him, and I called 911."

And that was the end of that. All the Morrisons had solid witnesses to their alibis for the time of the murder.

Ted turned back to Anne and Catherine.

"Anne, this is Ted Atkins, a reporter on our paper," Catherine said.

Anne reached from the stretcher where she lay to hold Ted's hand. "I know. We met before. Thank you. Catherine says without you I would have died. It is so lucky you were here."

A sob escaped her throat and her eyes filled with tears.

"You're welcome, Anne. I was only out here because I wanted to talk to you."

"As soon as I can, I'll call you," Anne promised.

Atkins watched the ambulance leave, feeling better about himself than he had since his wife and child had died. He shook his head as though clearing it of fog, got into his car, and drove away without another word.

A few hours later he finished two stories, all but the endings, one about the murders and blackmail, and the other, the scene at the bridge. All he needed were the endings and a conversation with Naomi Culver. He was sure his editor wouldn't run the first story without her permission as owner. He had no hope at all of David Culver allowing it.

Mrs. Culver agreed to see him that evening. Odd, he wasn't nervous this time. He waited for her in the small sitting room where he met her when he was hired. It seemed like an audience with royalty, that time.

But the lady who entered the room looked older, more tired and more worried than he remembered.

"Mr. Atkins, thank you for coming out here to visit me," she smiled. "What can I do for you?"

"My pleasure, Mrs. Culver. I wanted to show you two stories I have written for the paper next week. It's your paper and your family figures in the story."

"You wanted to give me a chance to kill the story?"

"No, I wanted you to know what's coming."

"And if I don't want them printed?"

"Then, I wouldn't work for you anymore, ma'am."

"I'd better read them."

She adjusted the reading glasses that hung from a delicate chain around her neck and read quickly, going back over an occasional paragraph. Finally, she put the papers on the pie crust table beside her, took off her glasses and rubbed her eyes.

"You write very well, Mr. Atkins. I hadn't noticed you writing at this level before.

"Thank you."

"You have handled the story as well as I could have expected. I would like you to publish both when you have the ends of the stories."

"And David?"

"What about me, Ted?" asked David as he entered the room.

"What if you don't care for what I have written?"

"What does Mother think?"

"I think they are first-class articles, David, and I think there has been too much secrecy."

"So do I, Mother. So do I. Publish, Ted."

"Thank you."

Ted shook hands with his employers and left, still dazed by the change in their point of view.

Chapter Thirty-One

A disgruntled group met at the police station the next morning. Adam explained to his near-drowned and head-injured workers that not only had the guy who assaulted them got away but he wasn't the one they were after for the murder.

"What the hell, Adam," Pete said, forgetting the office rule. "Why all the attacks on us if he didn't do nothing?"

"Fear for the wife, Pete. That's all."

"Are we going to let it go?"

"Hard to find him, if he went into northern Quebec where lived before, off the grid, so the brother said. Let's find this Ames woman."

Anne came in despite Catherine's entreaties to stay home in bed. She wanted to find the murderer, whom she blamed, somewhat irrationally, for all the things that happened to her. Anne's temper was slow to rise, but anger and determination to stop this person before someone else died replaced fear. After a few minutes of work, Anne found the reference. A manifest on the St. George, out of Bristol, listed a B. Ames. So Jennifer blackmailed Beatrice, too.

"Anne, do you think Jennifer would use *in.* to mean information, instead of using info?"

"She did try to be as obscure as possible."

Adam paced between his office and the main office, waiting for something he could work with.

"Boss, I found a Beatrice Ames listed in a phone directory for Littleton," Brad said.

"Can you find out if there's anyone else listed for the address? I'm looking for her mother, and I don't know her name."

"Sure."

He resumed his restless pacing. There was no lead to follow until Brad got him an address or a name.

"Boss, I got another name. Desiree Almonte lives at that street address."

Adam stopped his pacing. "See if you can find a connection between Beatrice and this lady and any of the people here."

"Why, Adam?"

"Just a hunch. Pete, you go down to Littleton and see if you can find the Ames woman there."

During the rest of the morning, Anne and Brad searched through Jennifer's databases, trying to construct a genealogical link between Beatrice Ames, Desiree Almonte and anyone else on the lists in Culver's Mills. Fed up with feeling like an extra thumb, Adam drove over to ask Ada Warren about this newest family on his list.

Ada worked in her garden, raking sodden leaves off her lawn and out from under bushes in the border around her property.

"Hello, Adam," she said. "You must be stuck for gossip again. Come in for a glass of lemonade."

"Hello, Ada. You're right about that. I hope you can go back about fifty or more years for me today."

Settling into a chair in Ada's kitchen, Adam explained he needed information about Beatrice Ames and another woman called Desiree Almonte.

"I haven't heard Desiree's name for at least forty years. That was a local scandal you know."

"What did she do?"

"Oh, it wasn't her. It was her mother. Desiree's name before she married was Dupre, and that was her mother's name. Her father couldn't or wouldn't give her his name. Desiree was always very ashamed. Imagine giving a love child a name like Desiree."

The old lady shook her head in disgust or amazement.

"Did Desiree have any family?"

"I don't know. She moved away before she married and never kept in touch with anyone here. I'm sorry Adam."

"No, thanks a lot. Just knowing her birth name will help Anne quite a lot."

"You persuaded her to stay, did you? Most of us thought you would."

"Do you mean my activities are common knowledge in your set?"

"Oh, now Adam, just those that are of any interest."

Ada beamed at him over her glass.

"I don't suppose you have any recent suggestions on who the murderer might be."

"Not that I've heard."

Adam said goodbye and walked down the path shaking his head. He was surprised Jennifer had kept her secrets as well as she had, considering Ada and her crowd.

The diner was clearing out after the lunch crowd when Adam arrived. Peg served behind the counter in spite of her new-found affluence. When he commented, she laughed and told him red tape took a lot longer than that to get through, and it would be a while yet before any money came her way.

After his lunch, Adam strolled back across the square to the courthouse. The sun was warm, birds were singing, flowers were starting to bloom in the beds in the square, and he felt oddly happy for a cop with an unsolved murder on his hands. The sight of Erin's shop told him why. The gone fishing sign hung from the door, so he walked on.

Anne and Brad were back from their lunch, and working on the information he had called them from Ada's. Anne told him she was constructing a family tree for the Culvers. She suspected Beatrice Ames might have been a twig from the family tree. Brad searched Jennifer's private databases for anything about Desiree.

Halfway through the afternoon, Brad called to Adam.

"Boss, I think I found something that might help Anne. It seems to be a copy of a birth certificate for Desiree. She was born here in Culver's Mills. The line for father is blank on this form, but Jennifer's notes say the original in Burlington lists the father's name. She identified him by one of those ship codes again. The initials are J.C., and the ship is the Galway again."

"Good. Anne, do you think you can do anything with that?"

"Yes, A Culver son born in 1900 was James. If we can find a James Culver or Calvert on the ship, I think you should try to look at the certificate."

As she spoke, Brad's fingers stuttered over the keys, calling up the ships' lists.

"Here he is. James Calvert shipped first class on the Galway in 1852."

"I think I should use a working theory that James had an affair with

Desiree's mother, and left her to raise the child alone. Maybe I can find some mention of them in the newspaper files. Ada said there was a marriage," Anne said.

"I need to know if there is mention anywhere of Desiree having a girl and if we can find her first name," Adam said.

"I'll look for that now," said Brad. "Have you heard from Pete?"

"Nothing yet. He's still at the address for Beatrice in Littleton."

By the end of the day, they were no further ahead. Pete staked out the house in Littleton, but there had been no sign of anyone, least of all Beatrice Ames. Adam told him to come in, leaving one of the county deputies on night shift.

Chapter Thirty-Two

The next morning was hopeful: no rain, a few pale streaks of sunshine and the warmest temperature in a week. Adam sent Pete back to Littleton, while the computers at the office were active again, looking for the tie between Beatrice and Desiree.

By noon, Anne found a reference in a *Births on Valentine's Day column*, to little Beatrice Almonte, the only baby born in Burlington on the saint's feast and how lovely it was for Desiree, her mother to have a baby on the day dedicated to love. Anne figured the writer must not have known the story of Desiree's own birth or she would have avoided the topic.

"Good job," Adam said. "As soon as I get word from Pete of any activity at the house, I'll go over. Is there anything more you think you can do?"

"Not with those records sealed. I don't know how Jennifer got her information unless she paid a bribe. The Vital Statistics office usually won't release anything about a living person without their permission." She paused before she went on to say, "She wouldn't have hesitated to bribe someone."

At that moment the phone rang. Pete reported that a grey Ford with two women, one quite old, and one answering Beatrice's general description arrived at the house. Adam told him to hold off approaching them until he arrived but to follow them if they left again.

Littleton was a small village. An abbreviated main street containing one each of the necessary stores: a grocer's, a vet, a pizza parlor and a small branch bank. Adam turned left onto Dayton Street and followed along until a sign pointed into a small cul de sac called, improbably, Strawberry Fields Way. Pete was parked at the entrance to the street.

"They're still inside, boss. It's the third house on the left."

"Okay, let's walk in. We'll leave the cars here. I don't want to cause too much of a fuss until we have to."

The small suburban house was set the required distance from the street, with an asphalt driveway, and a shrub on either side of the 'picture window. Adam could see the curtain move as someone watched their progress up the walk. When he rang the bell, Mrs. Ames opened the door. She was thinner than when he had last seen her.

"Come in, Lieutenant Davidson," she said. "I've been expecting you."

"Thank you, Mrs. Ames." Adam and Pete followed her into a small living room, crowded with the accumulated furniture of a lifetime. Before she sat down, Mrs. Ames handed Adam a clear plastic bag, with a heavy blue ball inside. He found the weight the same as the ones he had seen in the restaurant.

"You kept it."

"Yes."

Her face was older and more drawn than when he had seen her last, which must have been right after the murder. Waiting had taken quite a toll.

"Why?"

"If you had charged someone else, I would have come forward. I couldn't bear the thought that you might arrest an innocent person, especially one of the Culvers. They were good to me in their way." Her voice was almost inaudible, drained of all emotion.

"Is your mother here now, Mrs. Ames?"

"So you know that too. Dr. McPhail, I suppose. Yes, my mother's here. She's old, and I don't want you to frighten her. She had nothing to do with this at all."

An upright and almost fierce looking elderly woman entered the room in time to hear her daughter's words.

"That's not true, Beatrice. except for me, and my stupid pride, this never would have happened."

She sat down beside her daughter and took her hand.

"Beatrice only got mixed up with that woman because she was threatening to tell my story, and Beatrice thought I couldn't bear for it to come out."

"Can you tell me what happened? You know all your rights, but Pete will tell you again."

Pete pulled out his Miranda card and went over each item, making sure both women understood each one. Adam asked her again if she wanted to tell him, or after she had called a lawyer.

"I want to tell you now, Adam. May I call you Adam? It makes it easier somehow." When Adam nodded, she went on. "It all started one day about a year or a little less ago. I had just left a housekeeping job in Burlington and was looking for a new one. I had an ad in the paper. A woman called me, I thought in answer to the ad. That was Jennifer. She explained to me, very carefully and thoroughly that she knew all about the circumstances of my mother's birth, and she would make sure all my mother's friends would be informed if I didn't help her. I thought that would destroy my mother."

"She didn't want money?"

"Oh, no. She wanted me to take a job with the Culver's and gather information so she could blackmail them. She thought I should be happy to do this because the family had been so bad to my grandmother."

"Did she tell you what she was looking for?"

"Yes, she wanted anything anyone had to say about ancestors or old relatives. She wanted me to copy any old letters or documents I found. That was easy to do, because they have a copier in the office, and they're away a lot."

She paused for a long time, with her head down and her hands wringing each other.

"I did it. I found something about an Indian ancestor in an old letter. She took it, and by the way David looked from then on, worried and furtive, I knew she blackmailed him. It was awful to watch. I couldn't stop her blackmailing David, but I wanted out."

"So you met her at the library."

"Yes. The family was away that night, so I called her and arranged to meet her at 10:30pm. She thought I must have more information for her. When I told her I wanted out, she said not only was she not going to let me out, she wanted me to leave the Culvers and start on another family she had found that she thought had some deep secrets. I pleaded with her, but she turned away laughing and picked up the phone.

She asked if she should call Edith. Edith is my mother's best friend. I was so angry; I picked up the paperweight ball from her desk and hit her as hard as I could. I didn't mean for her to die, but I did mean to hurt her. How could I do it?"

Her mother stroked her hair.

"It was my fault, dear. I should have told you it didn't matter if the whole world knew, after all this time. I'm the one who's an old fool."

Beatrice went on, "I tried to erase the files, so all the awful information couldn't be used again, but I got frightened and ran away." At that, both mother and daughter started to cry.

Adam waited until they had stopped crying, and sent Pete for the car. He didn't feel there was any point in taking Mrs. Almonte with them to Culver's Mills, so they left her forlorn figure staring out the window after them.

On the way in he called the station. He wanted to give Anne the chance to leave. She would be very upset to see Beatrice.

Chapter Thirty-Three

A dam invited Erin and Anne and Brad to brunch at Catherine's. A now familiar figure got out of a car in the drive as Adam arrived. "Atkins, what are you doing here?"

"Hey, the lady invited me. She said you gave the okay to let me in on the end of this."

"I guess you write the story, now we have a confession."

Anne met them at the door and took them into the breakfast room. After brunch, a contented, well-fed and coffee-drinking group demanded an explanation from Adam and Anne.

"What happened, Adam?" Erin asked. "I thought you suspected the Beauchamps or the Culvers, and then the whole Russian thing happened, and now Beatrice."

"The two families were involved, but only because their ancestors lived here for so long."

He glanced over at Anne. "You tell this part."

"A Beauchamp's daughter, Leticia, married a Culver. This was the only time a Beauchamp's married locally. They jumped the gun a little, and a baby was on the way. When they died young in the influenza epidemic, the old grandmothers sent the child to New York. They had been embarrassed by the birth in the first place. After she grew up and married, her family had nothing to do with her and lost track of her descendants after she was murdered."

"Murdered. Did that have anything to do with this murder?"

"Not at all. It meant neither family knew Peg and May were their cousins. When we found the Beauchamps have a trust fund, we thought that gave Thomas motive for murder. However, he doesn't benefit from the trust himself, and they are intent on helping Peg and May. The next red herring was the whole Culver thing: first the rumor about the Irish maid, which wasn't true, at least not as far as we could find at the time; and then the aboriginal ancestor, which was. David Culver paid Jennifer to keep that one quiet. And you keep quiet, too, Ted."

"The Culvers gave me permission to publish the lot: murder, blackmail, everything."

"How did the Russian Mafia get involved?"

"That was Jennifer's bad luck," Adam said. "She discovered the Culver baby and the wills on both sides and also searched for land just like Anne did. When Jennifer found Howarth building on what was still Culver land, she and Davis started to blackmail him. This time she chose a real bad guy. Howarth was hiding from Interpol. He thought he might as well launder some money through construction. That was his style in Russia too: land that didn't seem to belong to anyone, a few bribes, perfect. Then came Jennifer. He had a genuine alibi for her murder because he didn't kill her. When he learned of her death, though, he took that as an opportunity to clean up the other loose end and get Davis off his back."

"What about the Morrisons?" asked Catherine.

"They're long gone into the wilds of Quebec, according to the brother. They had nothing to do with the murder. She was terrified ICE would find her."

"And all the time it was Mrs. Ames," Erin said.

"How is she, Adam?" Anne asked.

"Very remorseful. I think likely the charge will be reduced to manslaughter, but you never know."

"What about you, Anne? Are you going back to Canada tomorrow?" Erin asked.

"Are you going to continue your family research?" asked Brad.

Anne looked around the room. All these people who had become so close to her. So much to look forward to in their lives: Erin and Adam, Catherine and her boys. In almost losing her own experience here, somehow she recovered it. And now there was Thomas. Of course, she would return.

"I may give up genealogy forever. It is far too dangerous. Catherine has asked me to come back in the fall, so I hope to see you all then."

"For a quiet, uneventful holiday," said Catherine.

About the Author

Virginia Winters Murderous Roots is Virginia Winters" first published novel. Short works have appeared online in Camroc Press Review, Six Sentences, and Pine Tree Mysteries. A short story has been published in Confabulation2, an anthology produced by Wynterblue Publishing, North Bay, Ontario. Virginia blogs about writing and other interests, including genealogy, current events and gardening at her website, http://www.virginiawinters.ca. She also posts book reviews, and some of her photography. Virginia is a pediatrician, living in Lindsay, Ontario, Canada with her husband George, an internist, cat Fred and standard poodle Charlie.

Turn the page for and excerpt from the exciting sequel, The Facepainter Murders.

Sign-up here for my readers' group.

For more information or to contact Virginia
virginiawinters.ca
vwinters@bell.net

Sign-up here for my readers' group

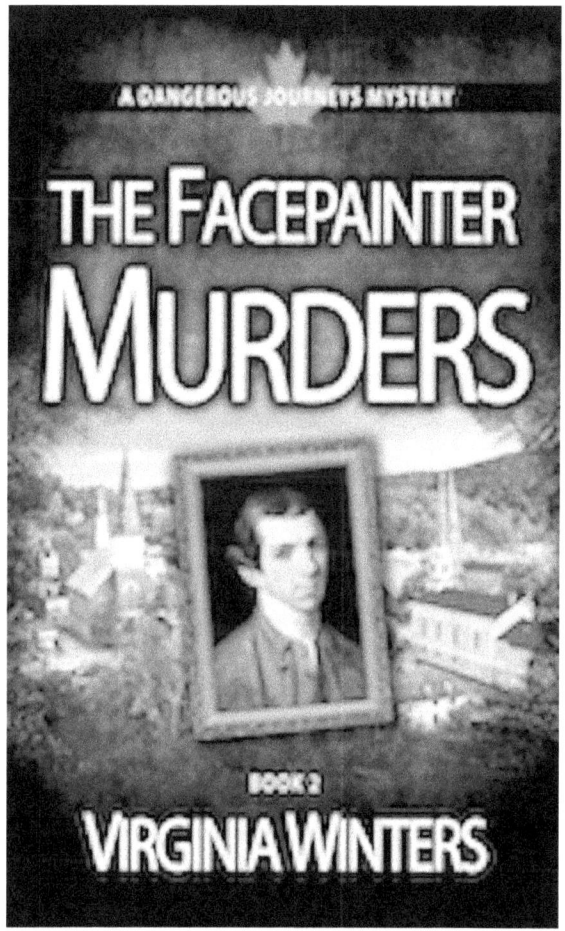

From The River Publishing

Cover Design by Karen Phillips

Dedication

For my family

Acknowledgements:

Thanks to my friend, Barbara McFadzen, for the many Friday nights she has spent listening to me while I read the latest story or chapter to her. Thanks are due to the Lindsay Public Library, reference division for its invaluable help. Finally, thanks to editor Shelley Rodgerson Chase for all the extra hours she spent on The Facepainter Murders.

C HAPTER 1

Maggie danced around the body that lay face down in the muddy water remaining in the ditch after the afternoon rain. Anne grabbed the dog's collar and dragged her away from her find. She must have smelled it all the way from the house, she thought. That's why she was so frantic to get out here.

She squatted by the head. A precise hole, just visible in the tangled mass of blood and hair, marked an entry point above the right ear. No point in touching him, she thought. No point but someone would ask if she had made sure he was dead. Her fingers felt through the water to where his carotid pulse should have been. Nothing. Nothing except that smell. Fighting the waves of nausea that threatened to overwhelm her, she wiped her fingers on the grassy bank and stood up.

"That's enough," she said to the protesting dog as she hauled her through the gate onto the path. Maggie tugged frantically the length of the garden and up to the kitchen door.

Catherine turned around from the stove, startled when the screen door slammed behind Anne.

"There's a body in the ditch," Anne gasped, as she collapsed into a kitchen chair, out of breath from her tug- of-war with the dog.

"Who?"

"I don't know. How could I know? I just got here; remember? Eighteen months since I was here last, and in all that time, did I find a body at home? No. Cross the border and here's another one, waiting for me in your back garden."

The ghost of a smile at the lame joke crossed Catherine's pale face as she said, "I'll call 911. No ambulance?"

"Yes, he's gone. So are all his clothes. Whoever left him there took all his clothes away."

"Naked?"

"Absolutely. I should go back. You're supposed to stay with a body."

Anne slumped against a pillar, watching the orange and black of an oriole as it darted at the feeder. The garden was a mass of scarlet and ochre with brilliant strokes of indigo from the butterfly bushes. Far better, she thought, to stay here. The dog whined softly from the other side of the screen door. Behind her she could hear Catherine speaking quickly to the 911 operator.

"No, Maggie," she said as she hung up the phone.

Anne forced herself off the porch and through the garden as far as the gate. She didn't go through, but stood looking at the fields while she waited for the patrol car and the questions. There would be many questions, that she knew. When she had found the murdered librarian on her last visit here, they had been endless. And then she had become involved with the investigation, and then she had almost died. Almost been killed. When she had finally gone home it had taken many months for the nightmares to stop.

She watched the body. The wind had picked up, rippling the water and giving an illusion of movement as it disturbed a few strands of the dark hair. She shivered in the sudden chill as the sun fell below the trees. The wail of a siren, rising and falling in the distance, came closer then stopped as a patrol car turned into the lane. The murky water, reddened by the flashing lights, lapped the body as though it steeped in its own blood. She shivered again as she turned to the voices of the policemen who walked towards her.

"Hi, Dr. McPhail," called the taller of the two men.

She recognized them as brothers Pete and Dave Graham. The one who spoke was Dave, the quieter younger brother.

"Damn shame you have to find a body every time you come down to see us," called the other, more lighthearted Pete.

"Was he dead when you got here?" asked Dave.

"Yes, he was. I could smell him," she answered, "and so could the dog. That's why I came back here. The dog. She wanted to see what it was."

"Do you recognize him?"

"No."

"How long have you been in the country, Doctor?" Dave continued.

"Since yesterday."

"We'll want to see your passport."

Anne could see Pete standing back as Dave asked the questions. Maybe he thought he knew her too well. She hadn't had much to do with Dave on her last visit. Everyone's a suspect until they're not, she remembered Adam saying to her.

"Okay, you go back to the house now. Adam will be along to speak to you," Dave said to her as Pete muttered into his shoulder radio.

"All right."

Anne walked back through the garden, not noticing the few flowers picked out by the last rays of the sun.

Catherine was pouring tea into gaily-painted ceramic mugs as Anne opened the screen door.

"Do you want to have something to eat while we wait for Adam?" Catherine asked.

"I don't think I can. How do you know I'm waiting for Adam?"

Catherine laughed. "It's a small town," she said, "and we have one detective who investigates homicides. Besides, when the patrolman reported who found the body, Adam would come anyway. After all the help you were to him the last time you were here, I'm sure he wants to see you again."

"Dave Graham didn't seem as friendly as last time. He seemed quite suspicious."

"Don't worry. Adam knows you."

"Yes, but two bodies in as many years?"

Catherine didn't answer, but turned to fill her teapot.

"What is it?" Anne asked, as she watched Catherine's fingers turn white where they encircled her cup.

"Not the best advertisement for a bed and breakfast," she answered, her eyes filling with sudden tears. "You know it's all I have and the twins are going away to school next year."

"I know." Anne remembered that Catherine's husband had died in the second year of their marriage, leaving her with the twins, the big old house and enough insurance money to bury him and get the business started.

"Should I go and look at him? What if he's someone I know? What if he's been a guest here?"

Now the cup was shaking. Anne reached over and held Catherine's hands. Cold, she thought. She needs that tea.

"Wait until they come and get us. Please drink your tea. You're very cold, Catherine."

An hour later, Anne was sitting in Catherine's little library, still waiting for Adam. She had left her little grey brick house in Bridgenorth, a small town in Ontario, the day before, leaving behind her Siamese cat, Albert. She had considered bringing him this year but wasn't sure how Maggie would feel about a cat invading her domain. Maggie sat on her footstool as usual, surveying her from behind grey bushy eyebrows. Half sheep dog, she seemed to need to keep all her humans in sight. When Adam came in she welcomed him with a few thumps of her slightly too short tail.

"Hey, Maggie," he said, rubbing her ears. "Hello, Anne."

His dark eyes and thin face looked more relaxed than last year, she thought, not as edgy. Maybe he was happier. Catherine had said that he was still seeing Erin, a local antique dealer.

"Adam, I didn't hear the door."

"I came through the kitchen. How are you?" "Not too bad, considering." "What did you see?"

Anne told him about finding the body. "…and Maggie pushed ahead of me, so there will be dog prints. I hauled her out of there as soon as I was sure he was dead."

"Did you see or hear anything else?"

"No." She went on, "We heard a car in the lane, before Maggie started barking, but I didn't see anyone when I went out."

Adam settled back in his chair and looked at her: small, early forties, very fair hair, green eyes set in a round face which bore an unexpected tan. She was a little thinner than last year, more grey in the fair hair, and a little tired-looking. Finding bodies could do that to you. He hoped neither she nor Catherine had any connection to the dead man. Anne was talking.

"It's good to see you again. I've been so looking forward to this trip. I hope that you'll have time to have dinner with me."

"I hope so too." He held out a small plastic bag with a torn scrap of paper in it. "Do you recognize this?"

"Is it part of a ticket? I've not seen one like that, but then I got here yesterday."

"We found it in the guy's hand."

"What a strange thing to hold on to."

Adam stood up. "Yes, it was. Catherine had to go look at the body. I hear them in the kitchen. Maybe she needs you," he said.

Catherine did indeed need her. Her thin body trembled and her large dark eyes held a film of tears. Anne sat with her arm around Catherine until she had stopped shaking.

"Catherine, did you know him?" Adam asked.

"No, I've never seen him before. So inhuman, somehow, to abandon him in a ditch." She looked across the table at Adam. "I don't think he's local."

"Neither do I. Thanks ladies, and thank you, Maggie," he said as he rubbed the ears of the worried-looking dog, sitting with her head on Catherine's knee. He walked out into the night and across the garden to where the crew was working.

Adam watched the forensics crew searching the lane and the roadside, moving like shadows in and out of the lights that had been set up around the scene. The body was dumped, he thought. Why would he have a ticket in his hand, especially if he saw the attack coming? What was the ticket for?

After a few words with Pete, he drove back through town to the police station.

The station was part of the courthouse complex on one side of the town square. Culver's Mills, population seventeen thousand, was a post-card-typical Vermont small town. The courthouse, clock tower and police station formed one side of the square. Opposite stood the white clap-board Methodist church. A short row of shops, including an antique store owned by Erin Maxwell—his own special lady—and professional offices filled in one side; a restaurant, homes and the bank, the other. Brick pathways crisscrossed a small green space, centered on a heroic statue of the town's founder. Quelling the impulse to stop and see Erin, he parked in front of the courthouse and took the ten steps to the door two at a time.

The police station occupied one wing of the courthouse building. The court's side was all polished marble floors and dark oak paneling, but once through the station doors only the bright screensavers on the desk computers enlivened the institutional-green walls, grey vinyl floors and steel filing cabinets. Four desks were jammed in the middle of the room. Cables, secured to the floor with duct tape, snaked around and between them.

"Brad," Adam called to his youngest officer, a computer expert.

"Yeah, boss." Brad was tall and loosely put together, his friendly nature showing all over his face.

"We have a problem. Our stiff out there has no clothes, no id. We'll need the fingerprints, dental impressions, maybe an artist. I don't think he'll photograph too well."

"I'll borrow from Burlington if we need one. Was there anything else at the scene?"

"Just this."

Adam showed him the torn ticket. He noticed now that the two letters remaining were Cu suggesting it was for something in town.

"Not like any ticket I've seen lately. I'll get a list of recent events from the paper and the rec center. Bars too. Sometimes they use tickets for special bands." Brad picked up his phone to start his round of calls.

"Circulate the motels and B and B's for missing guests and get the boys to check any vehicles that seem to be abandoned. I'm going over to talk to Peg."

"Will do." Brad grinned. Peg was the owner of the local diner, Lil's, and it was dinner time.

The diner was diagonally across the square from the courthouse in an old stone building that had previous lives as a lumberman's office and a grocery store. It had been Lil's for fifty years now.

Adam walked past the statue in the middle of the park, automatically touching the toe for luck as he passed, and up the stairs to Lil's door. Lil herself was long gone, but the décor remained the same. Red vinyl seats in comfortable booths filled the space in front of the windows on three sides. A white enamel counter, worn through to black in a few places, ran the length of the room. An old-fashioned, polished chrome milk shake maker stood at one end of the counter. Adam took one of the red and chrome stools and said hello to Peg.

"Hi, Adam—usual?"

Peg herself was thoroughly modern: close-cropped sandy hair, a pair of rimless glasses and a white shirt tied short over faded jeans.

"Sure."

Peg made the best chicken salad sandwiches, from her own home-reared and home-cooked chickens that he'd had anywhere, and he had tried them everywhere. He looked around the room, recognizing everyone except a family with two kids who were enjoying themselves, spinning around on the stools. No singles.

"So do you know who he is yet?" asked Peg quietly when she brought him the food.

"Don't tell me it's around already."

"Fraid so."

"No identification yet. Have there been many strangers through this week?" Adam asked between bites.

"A few. It's an in-between time. Most people were families or couples. Early in the week a guy was in here asking about art galleries and antique stores. I sent him across to Erin."

"What did he look like?" Adam asked as he reached for the catsup for his fries.

"About six feet, brown hair and eyes, small tight ears, straight nose, good teeth. Spoke well but he was pushy."

"Could be our guy. You don't remember a name or a vehicle?"

"Didn't hear a name and I didn't see him get in a car. He walked over to Erin's after his lunch."

"Thanks. How's your sister?"

Adam knew that Peg's sister May suffered badly from rheumatoid arthritis.

"Much better. Since we got the money from the trust, you know, we moved to the farm, all one floor and we got her some first-class care." Last year, as fallout from a murder case, Adam had identified May and Peg as beneficiaries of a local family trust.

"Has the family been decent?"

"Couldn't have been nicer or more welcoming. We keep a distance but they've been good to us."

"So why are you still here?" Adam asked, suspecting the answer he got.

"I enjoy it, especially the gossip," Peg said. Adam laughed, paid, and left to visit Erin.

The lights were on upstairs in Erin's building though the shop was dark. Adam went around the side and rang the bell. The intercom that he had insisted she install crackled a moment before he heard her voice asking who was there.

"It's me," he said with that softness that crept into his voice when he spoke to her. The lock snapped open as she told him to come up. He took the stairs two at a time to reach where she stood, silhouetted against the light from her apartment.

Erin was tall enough that her dark hair brushed his chin. Dark brown eyes accentuated the pale complexion of her oval face. Adam kissed her softly, and then they walked together into her apartment. Erin called it her loft although her bed was in a screened alcove and not visible from the living area. The large room took up most of the second floor of the house. One wall held a brick and tile fireplace surrounded by old pine bookshelves. Erin changed the furniture often, swapping pieces with her shop. Today she had a green corduroy overstuffed sofa and chair—his favorites.

"What's the matter?" she asked as she recognized his worried tension.

"You know Anne's here to visit?" As she nodded, he continued. "She's found another body."

"Oh, no. Who is it?"

"We don't know. He was naked and nothing was around him to identify him except this." He showed her the ticket fragment, but she shook her head slowly no.

"Peg said she sent a stranger who was interested in art galleries and antiques over to see you. Tall, she said, brown hair and eyes, pushy?"

"Oh, yes. He was in on Tuesday. I remember him because he demanded to see any paintings that I had stored away. I told him that what I had was in the shop and he was welcome to look. What I really wanted to do was throw him out."

Adam grinned at the thought of fierce little Erin throwing the guy out. Aloud he said, "Did you get a name?"

"John."

"Just John?"

"Just John. He didn't buy anything so I don't have a check or a credit slip or anything."

"Will you look at a picture when I get one? It won't be too nice."

"Sure."

Erin's face had grown paler. Adam put his arm around her and started talking about their upcoming vacation. In a few months Erin and he planned a trip to Bermuda — sun and relaxation and each other.

Their conversation was interrupted by a call telling Adam that the body was being moved from the crime scene to the morgue.

"Back to work," he said, as he got up from the sofa and stretched. A quick kiss and he was gone.

Also by Virginia Winters

The Deadly Arts Murders

Painting of Sorrow, book 1

Dangerous Journeys

The Facepainter Murders, book 2

No Motive for Murders, book 3

The Child on the Terrace, book 4

The Jewelled Egg Murders, book 5

Other works

A Superior Crime and other stories

All books available at Amazon sites worldwide.

If you enjoyed Murderous Roots, please leave a review at Amazon or Goodreads. Reviews help an indie author get noticed! Thanks.